D1431214

WALK IN THE MOONLIGHT

Books by Eve Bennett
April Wedding
I, Judy
Walk in the Moonlight

WALK IN THE
MOONLIGHT

BY EVE BENNETT

Julian Messner   *New York*

Published simultaneously in the United States and Canada
by Julian Messner, a division of Simon & Schuster, Inc.,
1 West 39 Street, New York, N.Y. 10018. All rights reserved.

Printed in the United States of America
Library of Congress Catalog Card No. 59–7010

For all the
Beloved Grandchildren

WALK IN THE MOONLIGHT

Mary Munday sat in study hall in Room 102 and, glancing out the window, thought that it was a pleasant spring day. She looked back at her *Scholastic Teacher* exercise without really seeing the lesson, which happened to be on the subject of United States newspapers. Her gaze wandered out the window again —Andy Bremer was just passing on the walk outside.

Mary's whole being suddenly prickled with something like shock, and she felt the hot color surge into her cheeks. And now, as Andy walked along, probably heading for the track field, Mary saw that this April day was beautiful, simply beautiful.

The softest of tiny breezes crept in through the opened casement of the window beside her, caressing her warm cheeks and stirring her hair. The sun was dazzling bright, the sky a brilliant blue. She saw in vivid detail every bit of the scenery that the window framed: the yard across the street where forsythia bushes sprayed their yellow gaiety, where spirea and flowering crab-apple trees budded in lavish promise. Daffodils and hyacinths rioted in borders along the walk. Nearby were several trees, their outlines rimmed with the most delicate of lacy green foliage. Even the nearest tree, close by the window, huge and gnarled and aged, was like a work of art with its black trunk out of which twisted silvery branches and baby twigs.

Mary laughed to herself. And blushed. Then she shook her head wryly. How funny that one boy's blond head and broad shoulders could highlight a whole landscape into sudden brilliance. It must be love, she thought.

She renewed her attack on the lesson before her with determination: "The ten United States newspapers which do the most responsible reporting are . . ." But her thoughts strayed out the window again, in spite of herself.

Mary was just seventeen this month, and her small feet had always before been planted quite sturdily on the ground. She had had boy friends, neighbors' boys, classmates, double dates. But she had also had heavier responsibilities than most girls her age, and her viewpoint was essentially matter-of-fact.

She wanted and liked dates, of course, and was thankful that she seemed to be popular enough, and good-looking enough, to be able to garner her share of attention. But she didn't sit around mooning about the matter, probably because she was always too busy to sit around mooning. Anyhow, never had anyone come along—until Andy Bremer—who did much of anything for her but give her some laughs and a date when she needed one.

Andy . . . She kept thinking about him after he had passed by, so tall in the sunlight, his blond head held high because he was a guy who knew where he was going and what he wanted. He was quite handsome in a clean-cut, square-jawed way. And the fact that he was one of Central's athletic stars accounted, probably, for the easy jauntiness of his walk.

Mary faced herself momentarily with the fleeting idea that maybe Andy's athletic popularity might explain some of her feeling about him. After all, he was one of the school's most sought-after boys. She brushed the idea aside quickly. Andy was the kind of fellow she had always wanted to meet.

Sometimes she wondered why he had picked her out to date, because all the girls hung around him panting . . . well, almost. And no doubt about it, a part, a very small part, of this ruckus in her girlish bosom was a feeling of being flattered because Andy had chosen her. They had been going steady for three months now. Three wonderful months.

Just the same, she defended herself, she had also chosen him, because she felt different with him from the way she felt with any other fellow. He's lucky I like *him* too, she thought . . . but didn't believe a word of it.

Mary shook herself. *The ten most responsible United States newspaper are* . . .

Silly, silly Mary Munday, the goon child of Eleventh Avenue!

After eighth period Andy came hurrying up to her locker. "Track," he panted, grinning. "Want to come out and watch?"

Mary shook her head ruefully, blushing and trying not to. "There is such a lot to do at home tonight," she told him, not quite wanting to remind him that she always did the washing on Friday nights when she got home from school. Then it would be drying Saturday morning and she'd have Saturday afternoon to do the ironing. Even now the wash was sorted out in discouragingly large piles all over the kitchen at home, lying in wait for her.

But she didn't tell Andy, who ran lithely in the spring sunshine, starring easily on the athletic field, while Mary Munday did the washing at home.

He squeezed her arm affectionately. "See you tonight then," he said, and was off down the hall.

Mary walked home that afternoon with two of her special friends, Barbie French and Tress Higgins, both of whom lived a couple of blocks further from Mary's home. The other two members of the select circle,

Lutie Phelps and Jodell Johnson, lived nearer the school and were staying for practice in the *a cappella* choir.

This was one of the first really warm and sunny days of spring, after one of Colorado's usual snowy, blustery Marches and a so-far-rainy April. The sudden turned-up heat of the sun, which was causing all the early blossoms and leafing trees to fairly leap into full bloom, had the effect of wilting the girls.

Mary sighed. "Gosh, I hate to go home to that old laundry."

Tress, whose mind was never on much of anything but dates and fun and boys, said, "You'll be all plumb wore out for your heavy date tonight."

Mary smiled and said, "No, I won't."

She turned in at her own walk and the other two strolled on. Though Mary's home was over fifty years old and not half as stylish as many others on Denver's east side—let's face it, not stylish at all—Mary loved the outside of the house. It was a tall old place of gray stone with white trim, a warmly mothering type of house, surrounded now by a whole belt of budding spirea, which within the week would make a frothy white framework. In winter the same bridal-wreath bushes surrounded the house with soft, snow-burdened branches and lights shining out of the front bay window at night cast a lovely glow on the white-laden bushes. Summer and winter, huge old trees spread their protective branches over the whole place.

As Mary entered the house, however, her feelings were mixed. The old-fashioned, high-ceilinged rooms represented a lot of day-in-day-out drudgery. The minute she stepped into the front hall, Mary became the lady-of-the-house, the home's only mother and wife, the maid-of-all-work.

Her mother had died at the birth of Stevie, Mary's young brother. In the ten years since that sad day, Mary and her father, big Jim Munday, had kept the home together.

Sometimes her father would say, "Mary, Mary, this place is too big for you to have to manage, too big and too run-down. We ought to sell it."

But Mary always stopped him. "It's our home," she'd say. "I don't want to sell it. I like it; I'm used to it. You care about it too." She did not remind him that they couldn't afford much better anyway. Small new homes might be 100 per cent easier to run, but they cost unbelievably more than big, ancient houses like theirs.

Mary was upstairs in her room, changing into faded washday blue jeans and shirt, when the banging of the front door announced the arrival of Stevie. No amount of reminding ever kept him from bursting into the house like a young tornado. His favorite answer, when Mary called to him as she did now, suggesting less noise, was "I was just comin' in, gee willikers!" This formality over, Mary said, "Hurry upstairs and get your pants changed. And that shirt is dirty; it needs to be washed. Come on, I need your help with the laundry."

"Aw, gee," Steve protested, clumping up the stairs, "the guys are waiting. We're going up to the reservoir and play ball."

"You're going to help me first, as you very well know," Mary said calmly.

When Stevie peered in at her door, scowlingly, Mary knew she loved the little scamp, even though they argued almost constantly. He was a small, slight boy, his shoulders thin under his shirt. He was big-eyed and freckle-nosed, with a shock of neutral brown hair that was always standing straight up, like a thick growth of wild bunch grass. There was something appealing about him—and yet he could be so maddening.

After a while Mary relented and let Stevie go tearing off to join his gang at the ball field. She carried the basket of wet laundry out to the lines and began to hang up the pieces in the late-afternoon sunshine. She glanced around the back yard; though not landscaped, it was wide and grass-carpeted, and surrounded by an aged, rustic fence. The clothes, smelling clean and fresh, blew lazily in the breeze, and Mary was conscious of a job well done.

Suddenly her eye caught a movement at the dining-room window of the house next door. That meant that

[15]

old Mrs. McDrey was peering from behind the lace curtain, looking for tattletale gray in Mary's wash, counting the towels and sheets, spying out every worn spot in every piece. Suddenly neither the washing nor the sunshine seemed quite so sparkling. Phooey on old, gossipy, prying, crabby neighbors!

When Jim Munday got home from work, Stevie was in the kitchen, his ball-field grime at least partly scrubbed off, his hair standing up or lying down in sporadically combed and wet-down spots, and Mary had the usual Friday-evening stew ready to serve.

Kissing her father, Mary knew that she was not as tired as he was. He looked exhausted. His faded blue eyes were often tired—but always kind. The many lines around his eyes and his wide mouth had once been laugh wrinkles—but now, in these older, hard-working, burden-bearing years, they marked the passage of time.

Big Jim Munday, they always called him. And he *was* big, six-foot-four and broad, but everything about him was gentle in spite of his size. He was a cement worker and there was always a grayness about him: in his hair, in the furrows of his face, in the callouses of his big hands. And his clothes were dusty with a light sifting of fine gray powder.

"Going out tonight?" he asked Mary, buttering a thick slice of bread. He worked hard and was always hungry at dinner. Finishing his first serving of stew, he refilled his plate with gusto.

When Mary nodded, he asked, "Andy?" and smiled.

"Yup," said Mary pertly.

"I like that boy," her father said. "He's a nice kid who'll treat my Mary right. Stevie, how about the show over at the Bluebird?"

"Sure, Pop," Stevie said. "I'll be ready in five secs."

"You don't need to gulp your food so fast," his father said. "I haven't had my coffee yet. And your sister will help you with the dishes. The show won't start till seven-fifteen."

Mary knew how thoughtful it was of her father to take Stevie to the movies. After his long day, he no doubt preferred to fall asleep over his newspaper after dinner. But the boy was only ten, and Mary and her father kept him in after dark, even though he often wanted to go out and wander around the neighborhood with his gang. They tried to provide amusement and interest at home, or accompanied him to a movie or a ball game. Neither Mary or Stevie had ever felt neglected by Big Jim.

"Maybe I'm a mite lenient with 'em," Mary had sometimes heard her father say to some eagle-eyed visiting relative, or overly helpful friend, "but you can't say they're spoiled. Mary takes care of the house beautifully and looks after her brother. And Stevie's just a normal, lively kid—I wouldn't want him any different. I mean to do the best I can for them."

Mary shooed her father and brother out of the kitchen with: "Your show starts earlier than mine. And

[17]

you know what a howling, pushing line-up there'll be. Gee, Dad, you're a brave man." Alone now, she breezed through the dishes and tidied everything before going upstairs.

After a shower, she dressed, wearing for the first time a blue cashmere skirt and a cotton Paisley blouse, also blue. The color did things for her blue-gray eyes, and the softness of the material accentuated the feminine lines of her figure. Mary surveyed herself in the mirror with approval. She was proud of the outfit, which she had just finished making. In order to save money and still have pretty clothes, she did her own sewing. She had worked hard in Mrs. Halvorson's sewing class at school, and tonight Mary felt she had profited well from her instruction.

She ran the comb through her soft brown hair, tied it back in a pony tail, and pinned a flower barrette around it.

She got out her coat, wishing she had a new short jacket and hoping that this three-year-old red one didn't look as threadbare as it had every right to be at its great age. She was ready for Andy when he drove up in his 1946 Ford station wagon jeep.

"Hi," Andy said.

"Hi." She slipped into her jacket, smiling at him. "I'm ready."

"You're mighty pretty too," Andy said.

They reached the downtown district and had to

make the usual circles around and around blocks, trying to find a parking place. The streets were full of young people, in couples and *en masse*, all in a noisy and gay mood: Friday night, and spring as well.

The film Mary and Andy wanted to see was at one of the big downtown theaters. The feature had been widely advertised and the place was crowded. Friday nights were not for older people—at least not those with frayed nerves and short tempers—for the young set was out on the town. In the movies they often expressed their approval or disapproval of the story with high spirits and loud comments. It was fun; nothing to bother anyone.

Later that night, on the way home, Andy stopped his jeep in the quiet solitude of Cheesman Park. Mary's heart raced; she *should* say, We must get home, it's nearly midnight, we shouldn't park . . .

She wanted to park. The night was full of magic, bright moonlight, and soft air. Besides, she had reason to trust Andy. Other than holding her hand in shows and a good-night kiss on most of their dates, Andy had not been too romantic, and that was all right with her. That was the way she wanted it. Only there was something in the air tonight . . . she wanted to park.

Andy sat quietly, gazing out over the park to the lights of the city below. Even the mountains, which formed Denver's skyline, were visible—remote and beautiful in this silvery night. Up near the winking red lights of a radio tower on Lookout, the tiny headlights of a car crawled along, circling some far-off high road. Mary sat very still too, her heart beating very fast. She hoped Andy couldn't hear it, but she was sure he could. He must ge able to feel it when he gently pulled her to him, so that she leaned against his chest, where his own heart was thudding. So they sat, watching the night's beauty, not saying anything.

Then, slowly, Andy turned her head with his hand and met her lips with a kiss that was soft, and yet his lips were firm. Mary usually shrank from the good-night kisses that most fellows seemed to think was only fair exchange for their evening's attention and money-spending—and maybe it was. The reason it had never seemed to be anything but a chore, to be done with quickly, was because Tad Shannon, the first boy who had kissed her, a couple of years ago, had lips that were too soft, like over-ripe fruit. Mary still shuddered when she remembered it.

But with Andy it was different. His kiss was firm and like himself, clean and nice. When he placed her head back on his shoulder, his arm around her tightened. They continued to sit in silence, one hand awkwardly stroking her hair. The smell of him was clean, and the hardness of his chest against which she leaned felt wonderful to her.

Suddenly he said, "We'd better go now," and started the car.

Kneeling by the window in her shortie pajamas that night, with her light out, Mary looked through the dark branches of her own special old elm tree. She breathed deeply. Such a wonderful evening. Such a wonderful world, full of beauty for the taking. She, Mary Munday, wanted to spend a whole long lifetime seeking out all the excitement and loveliness of such a world.

She was glad that Andy had kissed her just once tonight, a kiss that set her tingling from head to toes. One perfect kiss. And then he had held her, gently, tenderly. She knew by the way his heart had thudded that his feelings answered her own.

That was what had made the evening so perfect. They had shared it, they had known its magic. And then they had come home. And so it was something to remember . . . forever. Something to remember with happiness and no shame.

A beautiful, perfect evening in Mary Munday's life.

.... 2

Mary's Saturdays were enough to bring any girl back down to earth from the highest cloud. Some of the weekly cleaning chores she left until Sunday because, after all, there is just so much time and strength in one day. And on Sundays her father helped her with the heavier work.

Stevie lent his so-called help on Saturdays, but Mary often felt that it took more effort to make him work than it would take if she did the things herself. After she got the laundry sprinkled for the afternoon's ironing, she scrubbed the woodwork where it was needed most (she *despised* woodwork scrubbing), mopped the kitchen and bathroom, and did baking enough to last the next week.

The ironing was one of the household tasks she most hated. Usually, no matter how hard you try, the darkest, dreariest thoughts seem to attack you over an ironing board; while aches and stiffness spread from your feet up into your back and shoulders.

[22]

Today, however, Mary thought she didn't mind as she moved about the kitchen. "Reminds me of the kitchen we had on the farm," Jim Munday always said, "with my mother's rocker all homelike-looking at the window—only the kitchen took so much work she never got to sit in the rocker much. These big old kitchens look picturesque, Mary, but I wish we could have a small modern one for you."

Her father had installed such modern gadgets as they could afford: a refrigerator, a fairly good electric washer, a new and bigger sink. Mary never dreamed of fancier things, partly because she had never used them; and partly because she only dreamed of getting out of the kitchen as fast as she could.

That was why she had firmly resisted taking the cooking class at school which her sponsor, Mrs. Donner, had suggested. Much as she liked the cooking teacher, Mrs. Harrison, Mary had more than enough of cooking at home, thank you.

This morning, she breezed through her work.

"What's with you?" Stevie demanded, squinting at her suspiciously. "What're you grinning about all the time? Something funny? I don't see anything funny around here. Gee willikers, I've cleaned my room till it shines."

Mary grinned. "Everything safely tucked under the bed?"

"You can go and see for yourself!" Stevie announced, loudly. "Can't I go out now?"

"Okay," Mary said. "Run along."

Her small brother stared. "Now I *know* something's the matter!" But he grabbed up his softball and ducked out the door before she changed her mind.

Mary went on rolling out pie dough while her brother dashed up the alley, headed for the reservoir and the lot where the neighborhood children played.

Her nimble fingers were expert with the dough. It was just as well, this morning, for she was absent-minded, her thoughts obviously not on proportions of flour, shortening, apples, sugar and cinnamon.

A light breeze played in and out of the open window beside Mary's work space. A robin sang his heart out in the branches of the cherry tree outside; singing, Mary thought, sentimentally, to his mate. Mary was in love. In love with spring, in love with life, in love with love. In love with Andy.

She was cleaning up the kitchen when she heard the voices. One was raised and angry, the voice of Mrs. McDrey next door; and the other voice was Stevie's, shrilly defending his rights.

Mary rushed to the kitchen door. Old Mrs. McDrey, who lived alone, stood on her side of the fence, clutching Stevie's ball in her gnarled hand. Stevie, on his side of the fence, was white behind his freckles, but fiercely defiant.

The woman saw Mary in the doorway and cackled, "I've told your brother I'd keep any ball he threw over into my yard! I don't aim to have him trampling my lawn and flowers all the time. I've told him a hundred times. He broke my big window last year, as you very well know, and he's bothering me all the time——"

Mary descended the steps and went over to the fence. Over and over their father had told them to try to get along with Mrs. McDrey, never to talk back to her. "She's old and sick," their father said. "And you've got to learn to get along with people. Steve, you stay out of her yard."

"I don't want to go near her old yard," Steve always broke in here. And Mary would add, "The Sowers sisters, on the other side, have a nice yard too, and we get along with them. When Stevie climbs on their fence or loses something in their yard, they're nice about it. A person *feels* like cooperating with them."

Their father always went steadily on. "Don't throw your ball near anyone's yard nor climb on anyone's fence. Mrs. McDrey works hard and keeps her yard nice; you can't blame her." And then he'd repeat the code he wanted them to learn: "You've got to learn to get along. Your rights stop where the other fellow's begin. If you don't bother Mrs. McDrey, she won't bother you."

Now Mary took a firm grip on her quick temper. She resented the old woman's carping voice, her angry face. She resented anyone who made Stevie look so scared. She tried to speak quietly. "Mrs. McDrey, I'm sorry Stevie's ball got into your yard. He knows he mustn't go in after it without asking you. If you will give it to me, please, I'll see that he doesn't play ball on this side of the house."

"That's what you always say!" the old woman cried. "But it always happens again!"

"Boys have to play ball, Mrs. McDrey," Mary said, hoping she sounded composed, which she didn't feel. "It's as natural as it is for you to grow flowers."

"I don't bother him with my flower-growing," Mrs. McDrey retorted with horrid logic. "I want him to stay away from my yard!"

"I promise you he'll stay away," Mary said. She was furious and the hand she extended for the ball was shaking. The old woman scowled but reluctantly handed over the ball. "Next time I keep it!"

"*Stevie!*" Mary warned, for the face he was making was not what you'd call respectful. His features snapped into place before Mrs. McDrey saw him. Mary handed him the ball. "Go to the other side of the yard!" she said sternly. "Why couldn't you stay up at the field and play?"

"Because," Steve pouted aggrievedly as Mary walked beside him, "by the time you let me out, all the kids were gone. Aw heck, my whole day's shot."

Mary rumpled his hair. "Come on in," she said. "I've just taken cookies out of the oven and I'll make you some lemonade. How about it? You look hot."

"That old bat makes me hot," Steve growled, but his face lighted up as he followed her into the house willingly.

The day wasn't shot as far as Mary was concerned; though certainly some of the shine was rubbed off because of the scene with the quarrelsome Mrs. Mc-Drey. Why must people want to make trouble for other people? Particularly for sensitive little kids? Such a nice world, such a short life to be lived . . .

For the afternoon she had a large ironing to do. But tonight she had another date with Andy.

After lunch, when Stevie set off bicycle-riding with his pals, Mary set up the ironing board with fair good will. She could forget how she hated doing so many shirts, while she remembered some of the fun she and Andy had had together. They'd gone dancing several times. Mary loved to dance and she thought she wasn't too bad. Naturally, Andy was better. He seemed to do everything well, and his athletic prowess had made him extremely graceful on his feet.

. . . One snowy March night a gang of them had hired a hayrack from Glasier's barn and had gone for a ride and then returned to Glasier's for a campfire. Oh, that had been so much fun. But most of all, she thought she enjoyed the times when just the two of them were together, talking, laughing, being good companions . . .

[27]

The scorched place, thank goodness, was on the long tail of one of her father's work shirts!

She had a picnic supper ready for her father and brother that night at five-thirty. Potato salad, hamburgers on buns, pickles, her own concoction of baked beans with molasses, bacon, and catsup, then cookies and iced tea. She served her two men out under the trees—their first back-yard picnic of the year. There were no dishes to do!

Then she changed into her newest pair of blue jeans, her brightest plaid shirt, a red scarf around her hair, and her beat-up leather jacket. Basket packed, she was waiting for Andy when he arrived at six. Tonight was to be the first steak fry of the season in the mountains.

Mary felt just a twinge of guilt as she waved good-by to her smiling father. For all his kindliness, Jim Munday had some old-fashioned ideas to which he adhered with unswerving tenacity. One of his rules was that Mary should not, at any time, go alone into the mountains with any boy. Not even with Andy, whom he liked.

However, a steak fry, with a gang, was different, Mary rationalized. If he knew, though, he might still worry about lots of things, about the hazards of mountain driving at night, for instance. He still remembered his own boyhood in these same Colorado mountains and what it was like to be sitting around a campfire at night . . . Mary sometimes caught a fleeting glimpse of concern in his eyes; but he said it himself, kids have to have fun and you have to trust them. And she was trustworthy.

Mary knew she wasn't playing fair with her father tonight. He hadn't asked—because he trusted her—how many others were going along. He probably assumed that Andy, after picking her up, would fill the jeep to overflowing. And a father could take his choice of things to worry about: the danger of an overloaded jeep on mountain roads and a hilarious, perhaps careless, bunch as opposed to the dangers of a boy and a girl alone up in the mountains at night.

Tonight, only Andy's pal, Frank Harrell, and Frank's girl, Marcia Bassett, were going on the steak fry. They were going in Frank's car, and Mary and Andy were taking the jeep.

Mary thought that if she explained to her dad, he might understand, at least he would if she talked it out with him. But it would only worry him a bit more than necessary. Actually, she was conforming to the letter of the law. And how could she explain to him that she was safe with Andy?

How could she put into words that wonderful feeling of last night, how good, how nice, it had been? Parents only see the fact that somewhere there is danger for their children, that they must be shielded from it. So Mary didn't go into details with her father.

She just promised herself that she would see to it that, as always, she was a good girl. She smiled at Andy as she climbed into the jeep, trusting him and his nice smile and his little old jeep.

The jeep took the climb up Turkey Creek Canyon like a gay mountain goat. After a long ride, they turned off onto a side road leading to a place that Frank had assured them was the best picnic spot in the whole front range of the Rockies. Next they climbed a high, rather narrow road for several miles before sighting a wide, grassy, tree-shaded grove near a meandering, pebbly stream.

Frank and Marcia—who had been going steady for well over a year and who, Mary sometimes thought with a trace of disapproval, acted almost like a pair of honeymooners—had arrived ahead of them and had the fire started. A wilted bouquet of early wild flowers lay on a nearby rock.

The boys had furnished the steaks and the girls had brought buns, potato chips, pickles, and whatever else they could think of. Mary had put half her home-baked beans in a stone pot and brought them along, as well as some of her fresh cookies. Frank had brought a portable icebox, and the Cokes from it were frosty.

So far above sea level, a warm April day can change fast into a nipping, chilly night, and the fire felt good as they hovered around it, preparing the food. Never were steaks so delicious as those with singed edges and raw centers, fried on a mountainside by starlight.

They at omniverously, then built up the fire and sat around on spread-out army blankets, singing and talking lazily. Mary leaned back against Andy again and felt content and happy. She tried to ignore Frank and Marcia and their giggling and whispering. They were silly, and that's a fact. Mary was glad that she and Andy . . .

A phrase crossed her mind, *God, I thank Thee that I am not as other men* . . . and she grinned at herself.

Her father, trying always so painstakingly to raise his children correctly, read them the Scripture every Sunday at breakfast and then discussed with them what he had read, to make sure they got the meat of it. Some of the discussions waxed quite unorthodox, what with Stevie's piping questions, some of Mary's flat challenges, and Jim Munday's earthy attempts at explanation. They may have ended up with an unconventional picture, but they got the idea. After one such discussion Mary had clearly visualized the old Pharisee, a white-bearded old man, tromping up the temple steps and praying for the world to hear, "God, I thank Thee that I am not as other men."

She knew people like that. "Just be sure you never get the idea you're better than everyone else," her father had warned.

So, too, she had formed a unique idea of the older brother of the Prodigal Son as a jealous, small-minded fellow, resenting the fact that his younger brother had the get-up-and-go to want to see something of the world, to get out on his own for a while. Now, she thought, I am not as silly as Marcia, thank goodness, and Andy and I wouldn't . . . Old Pharisee Mary Munday.

These thoughts had brought her father to mind. "Let's go home," she said.

It was about nine-thirty when they put out the campfire. They waited a few minutes, to be sure every last ember was burned out. Andy was very particular about this. The night wind whipped them now, and they stood close together, growing chilled. Beside them the little brook melodied sleepily over stones. The stars up there seemed very close and very brilliant.

Frank and Marcia piled into their car and set off first. "Did you have the feeling we were intruding on their privacy?" Andy asked. "I guess they want to do some heavy necking before the evening's over."

"Heavier than *that*?" Mary sniffed.

Once in the jeep, she put her head back on the seat. Andy began to hum, one of the tunes they'd been singing around the campfire, and she joined in. "There's a Gold Mine in the Sky . . ."

The canyon walls loomed steep and dark on both sides, but the road was a ribbon of moonlight straight ahead, and the stars high above were like friendly lights winking down at them.

[32]

Another beautiful night. Another wonderful time with Andy.

They had dropped gradually down the road for a distance of several miles when without any warning the jeep coughed and seemed to lurch. It seemed to be holding back as Andy pumped the accelerator. He muttered, "Oh-oh!" as the car moved slowly forward until the engine spluttered and died.

Mary looked at him. Andy pushed the starter. The motor turned over, coughed—and died. With each try the motor seemed farther from catching, until pressing the starter produced nothing but a feeble purr.

Andy muttered something under his breath. "I knew I should have checked that carburetor," he said aloud.

"Can you fix it?" Mary asked, trying to conceal her worry.

"It might possibly be the fuel line. I can fix that. But I'm afraid it's the carburetor. It's been acting up lately."

Andy reached into the glove compartment for his flashlight, then climbed out and lifted the hood. For what seemed long moments he tinkered with the car's innards. By the light of the flashlight he took out a line and blew through it. Finally he seemed to be readjusting parts as he had found them. Then he leaned against the fender and stared at the engine.

"Yup, it's the carburetor," he said in a disgusted voice.

"What can we do?" Mary asked, climbing out onto the road to stand beside him.

"If we could get a push, it would start, I think. We might be able to keep it going into town, since it's all downhill. At least it would go till we have to stop for something. But that would be quite a fire risk. See how the gas is leaking?"

He turned the flashlight beam onto an object protruding from the body of the engine. It appeared to be covered with fluid. "Nope," Andy said with finality. "We aren't going anywhere in this car tonight."

"Maybe," Mary offered timidly, peering down the steeply embanked sides of the road, "maybe I could steer and you could push . . . ?"

She was being very brave. But Andy, absorbed and mad as a man can get with a car, snorted: "Heck, no! Want to get us killed? I'm afraid it won't run anyhow. We'll just have to sit here and hope that someone comes along."

They sat. At first there was the cold white moonlight above the darkening canyon walls. Then the moon hid behind a cloud and there was only the chill wind and darkness.

Andy fumed at first, but then he noticed that Mary was shivering and her eyes were large and very serious. He put his arm around her. "I'm sorry, kid. Surely someone will come along soon. There were other picnic parties when we came up."

They waited a while longer, and Mary decided that they must be the only people around for miles. "Andy," she said at last, "there might be quite a lot of traffic on the main canyon road, but we turned off, remember? I think Frank and Marcia must've chosen that spot because it was so remote. Maybe—maybe we ought to start walking?"

"Oh, there'll be a car coming any moment," Andy said impatiently. His voice sounder very young and cross and uncertain.

They sat and waited. No car came.

Andy sighed loudly. "Okay. Let's start walking. It's too cold to sit here any longer. It's a good five miles down to where we turned off. I sure hope we don't have to walk that far."

Mary clambered out behind him. They started to walk at a brisk pace because they were cold. They were silent for quite a while. For more than one reason Mary's teeth were chattering so that she didn't think she could talk if she tried.

At every sound behind them they both jumped and turned. Maybe a car was coming? Maybe something else?

Finally Andy halted. "Hey!" he cried, abruptly. "You're limping! What's the matter?"

"Oh," Mary explained apologetically, "I'm wearing

loafers. I should've known better, coming into the mountains. But I didn't think we were going to do any climbing . . . or anything."

"Or walking miles," Andy said bitterly. "Gosh, Mary, I'm sorry about this. Why don't you sit down and rest a while?"

"Oh, no," Mary said quickly. "It's too—it's too cold. I'm all right."

She took Andy's arm and limped on, stopping for short periods to rest her feet. She was sure there was at least one blister on each heel, as they continued down the road it became very painful. Andy led her to the side of the road. "Come on, we're going to sit a while," he said firmly. "You poor kid. I could kick myself for not having that carburetor adjusted. My Dad's always told me—— Hey, suppose I could carry you for a while?"

Mary laughed in spite of the predicament they were in. "My hero! You may be the athletic type, my boy, but you're not Atlas! *No!*" she insisted as Andy made threatening motions of picking her up. "I tell you, if you've got a big handkerchief, I think maybe I could wrap it around this sore place and it would be okay. I was so silly to wear such loose shoes."

Andy produced his handkerchief and Mary wrapped up the blistered place, not telling him that the loafers were all she had to wear for such occasions as picnics.

They walked on slowly, and covered five miles before turning into the main canyon road. Still no cars came, so they continued to walk, very weary now. Never had there been such a quiet night in Turkey Creek Canyon.

"Is everybody dead?" Andy said. "I'm beginning to feel as if the end of the world has come and we're the only two left alive."

Mary shivered. "Ch-Cheerful, aren't you? I keep wondering if it won't be daylight soon."

"Oh gosh, no," Andy said bluffly. "It just seems long but I don't imagine it's really very late."

"My poor father," Mary whispered. "He'll be so worried."

"My folks will be too," Andy said glumly. "And my Dad will be sore because I didn't have the car checked before we started."

Suddenly there was the unmistakable sound of a car engine behind them. They stopped and began waving frantically. The car was roaring as it descended the twisting canyon road at a terrific rate of speed. They could see, as it flashed past, that it was some sort of a sports model.

"At least," Mary said, "we now know that we're not the only ones still alive on earth!"

"They won't be alive long," Andy said savagely, "going like that. They nearly ran us down."

"There'll probably be another car along soon," Mary comforted him. "And not many drivers would pass up a couple of kids on foot on a mountain road."

The next driver—half an hour later—stopped. To them he looked like an angel, peering over his glasses out the window of his light truck.

"Want a lift?" he inquired cheerfully. "I go as far as Morrison. Out kind of late, ain't you?"

They climbed into the truck hastily and gratefully. Andy explained their troubles as they drove on with the old man. Although they could at last rest their feet and the old man's company was a comfort, they weren't making such progress, for the little truck skittered along at about twenty miles an hour.

Quite a few other cars began to pass them now, but they didn't want to appear rude by asking the old man to let them transfer to faster transportation—provided, of course, that faster transportation would pick them up.

"Joe's Garage is open all night," the old fellow told them. "Likely you can get him to go back up after your car for you."

When they finally arrived in front of Joe's Garage, it was closed up tight, with no sign of lights or life. "Oh, say, now I remember," their charioteer remembered, "Joe's mother's real sick back in Saginaw, Michigan. He left today on the bus. Well, I'm sure sorry, kids. I'd like to take you further, but I'm late home now."

"That's all right," Andy said. "We appreciate your

bringing us this far. We'll soon get another ride, I know. How much do I owe you?"

The driver waved his hand. "Not a cent, not a cent! I liked having company. Good luck!"

Out on the road again, they were picked up quite soon. This man, not nearly so garrulous as the truck driver, took them to the end of a bus line on the edge of Denver. "I think this line runs all night," he told them and sped away.

Fortunately the buses on that line did run all night— but not often. Finally one came along and it took them down to the heart of town where they could connect with a bus that ran only every hour. They had evidently missed the last one by a matter of minutes. At close to five o'clock in the morning, by the Daniel and Fisher's tower clock, they took a Number 14 bus, which would bring them near Mary's home.

Andy walked her the four blocks from Colfax to her house. He had eight blocks more to walk to reach his house. Birds were chirping sleepily, the sky was lightening overhead, and the milkman was coming down the street when they arrived at Mary's door.

The drapes were pulled open in the bay window as Mary approached the house at about twenty minutes before six that Sunday morning. She knew then that her father was up.

"Want me to go in with you?" Andy offered.

"No, oh no," Mary said. " 'Bye. I'll see you."

The door was unlocked and she went in quietly but hopelessly. Her legs were trembling with weariness, with nerves too. Sure enough, her father sat in the big chair facing the window.

He was sitting there in his old green bathrobe, and his face was as gray as his hair. His big hands hung between his knees as though he didn't care to hold them up. He gazed at Mary wordlessly. And he looked tired, tired, tired.

Mary rushed across the room and fell to her knees before him, throwing her arms around him. "Oh, Daddy!" she cried. "You look so tired and you've been so worried! I'm all right. I'm so sorry I frightened you, but there was no way I could avoid it. Honest, the car broke down and we waited and waited for someone to come by. We were way up a canyon off Turkey Creek . . . and *no* one came along—we had to walk *miles*. We didn't get picked up till we got a few miles the other side of Morrison, and then we had to hitch another ride and come home clear across town on buses. That's what happened, Daddy, honest! I didn't telephone because I hoped you'd be asleep and wouldn't be worried."

He looked down at her and then asked slowly, "Couldn't you have come home in someone else's car? Did you all ride in one car?"

Mary faced him. "There were only two cars, Daddy. Frank and Marcia went on ahead in theirs and never knew we were stalled." She looked at him squarely. "Andy and I went alone in his jeep."

"But, Mary, you know——"

"I know," Mary said. "It was cheating, only it seemed like such a tiny thing. And now I'm so ashamed. I should have known it wouldn't turn out right. I'll never cheat you again, Daddy, if you'll believe me and forgive me this once."

"Of course I believe you," he said. And proved his trust by adding: "I thought some accident must have happened. I guess I'm like a broody old hen. I knew you wouldn't stay out like this otherwise; you've always been dependable. I called all the hospitals. Somehow I couldn't quite call the police about one of my kids."

"Oh, Daddy!" Mary cried. "I'll never, never do this to you again!"

Her father laid his hand on her head. "You must be awfully tired. Get some sleep. We can talk later."

"Did you get any rest?" Mary asked. "This is Sunday, the one morning you can sleep!"

"I'll nap this afternoon," her father said. "Right now I think I'll get dressed and work in the yard."

Andy called that evening, a hurried, low-voiced call. "Oh yes, my folks believed me all right," he said shortly. "But they were sore just the same, because they were worried. I guess that's the way parents are. My Dad and I went up and got the jeep today and towed it down to the garage. So he knew it had quit running all right. He seemed to think I should have managed better, just the same. And of course he had told me always to check before I took the car out of town. He said if I was going to be stupid about things, I'd better not go into the mountains again till either the jeep or I was more responsible. I've got to go now, Mary. The folks are sort of edgy tonight and they reminded me I've got studying to do. See ya——"

Mary was still exhausted on Monday morning, and went through the day in a trancelike state, reciting only when called upon, studying without absorbing, quiet when she was with a group at lunch hour.

She passed Marcia Bassett in the hall and Marcia came running over to her, eyes sparkling. "He-ey, what's this I hear? Out all night! Naughty, naughty! And actually"—Marcia giggled, batting her black eyelashes—"I'll bet Frank and I got in more necking than you did, and we were home by two o'clock. Our folks were asleep, and nobody the wiser."

"We didn't have our minds on necking," Mary told her. She didn't like Marcia much.

Marcia said, "Just between you and me, I don't think Andy'll ever have his mind on necking. He's a cold potato . . . out for himself, if you know what I mean."

"I'm glad," Mary said shortly, and walked away. She was to remember this conversation in later months.

Mary told her friends, Jodell, Barbie, Lutie, and Tress, about the whole evening, the whole night, as they met outside the school after eighth period. She told it all—how she'd not quite told her father the truth, how he'd worried all night, how ashamed she was. "I'll never do anything like that again," she vowed.

"It could happen to anyone," Jodell said. "It was bound to happen when you weren't quite on the up and up. Be sure your sins will find you out, they say."

Jodell was the same age as the rest of the group, but

[43]

she was more like a big sister. Mary leaned on her in place of the mother she missed. Jodell, plain-faced, tall, and broad-shouldered, with her dark hair drawn back tightly in a pony tail, was sensible and outspoken. She didn't have many dates, but she advised the rest of them with theirs, helped in every way she could, and seemed to have an endlessly patient generosity as a mother confessor.

Lutie was the quietest one of the five of them, quiet and sweet and shy. She was a pretty, rather fragile-looking girl. Even more fragile-looking, however, and certainly very pretty, was Tress, whose blonde-brown hair had a way of breaking out in soft curls all around her heart-shaped face; and whose blue eyes were bright and restless, always in search of excitement. "Tress looks so fragile," Jodell had once remarked, "and actually she's about as fragile as a large charge of electricity."

And then there was Barbie, who was striking-looking and who, as one of seven children, had learned to be a good sport and a gay addition to any group.

The week dragged on, one of those humdrum weeks where nothing seems to go very right or to matter very much. The weather was suddenly unseasonably warm, and studying in crowded classrooms became quite dull, in fact almost impossible.

Mary didn't see much of Andy all week. They never

dated during the week unless it was for a Coke after school or an occasional evening's study together. This was another rule of Mary's father, and she went along with it willingly, because she didn't have the time. With all she had to do, her studies would certainly suffer if she went out on week nights.

Andy was busy preparing for a regional track meet, and he just didn't see Mary much, except for a brief meeting or two in the halls at school. He still seemed a bit concerned about his parents' reactions to the events of last Saturday night. And it would take forty-five dollars, he reported gloomily, to get the jeep fixed.

On their movie date the next Friday night Andy was still acting depressed. The jeep was still in the garage and he seemed to feel that he was disgracing Mary by asking her to ride the bus.

"No matter what you read about us modern juvenile delinquents," Mary told him, "there are a lot of us girls who don't mind riding buses. I'm used to it."

"Well, I hate to be without the jeep anyhow," Andy said grumpily. "I'm so used to it, I don't feel right without my hand on the wheel. And, gosh, I'll be broke forever, paying that garage bill."

"Maybe you could ask the driver to let you take turns driving this bus," Mary teased him, "so you'd feel at home."

Andy was not amused. "Parents are the darndest people," he went on. "My folks say, sure, they believe

[45]

me. They have to believe me, because Dad had to tow the jeep down last Sunday and he saw for himself it couldn't run. But all week they've acted like—well, as though it must be all my fault. It certainly wasn't anything I dreamed up. Dad was stalled on a selling trip up in Wyoming in that blizzard last winter, and was about twenty-four hours late getting home. And *he* was a big hero; nobody acted as if it was all his fault."

"Maybe," Mary said, smiling at him, "maybe the difference is that they suspect you might have *liked* to keep me out late."

He grinned at her suddenly. "Gosh, you're sweet, and such a darned good sport. I'll always remember how game you were, walking those miles down that mountain road without grumping at all. I'll bet your legs still ache. And how's the blister?"

"I'm fine," Mary told him. "It's one of those things you have to experience so you can look back on it and laugh when you get old and gray. It would be awful not to have anything to look back *on* and laugh *at*."

Andy squeezed her hand and was cheerful for the rest of the evening. On the front porch that night he reminded her that he had to go to the track meet at Boulder the next day, and probably wouldn't be home early enough in the evening for them to go out.

"That's all right," Mary said. "I need some extra time to cram for that Western History test. Why, oh why, can't I remember dates?"

"I'll bet there's one date you'll never forget," Andy grinned.

And Mary said, "I certainly won't."

She was to recall that remark later too. But now she had the sudden bleak thought that sometimes there was a dance after the track meet. Andy didn't want to be tied down to her for that evening, he might want to stay in Boulder . . .

But Andy called her at a little after nine the next evening. "Want to go out for a Coke or something?" he asked.

Mary said, smiling contentedly to herself, "No, I thought I'd be staying home so I washed my hair. Tell me about the meet."

So, over the phone, Andy reported, "I won the hundred. Came in second in the two-twenty low hurdles. I think I might have won it too, but I got off to a bad start. Central finished second in the meet."

On Sunday night Mary and Andy went to a potluck supper given by the young peoples' church discussion group.

The next week went slowly too. Mary thought she must have spring fever *bad*. She had a lot of studying to do; she was trying to get some sewing done at home . . . and, somehow, everything seemed to drag.

And then came Wednesday. At noon, in the lunchroom, Tress brushed past and said conspiratorally, out of the corner of her mouth, "Got something to tell you after school."

Since Tress was a great one for finding excitement wherever she could, Mary didn't think much about it. It was probably some silly idea that didn't amount to a hill of beans . . . a new fellow Tress had met, probably.

Tress, Jodell, and Barbie were waiting for her after school on the south walk. "Come on over here," Tress said mysteriously. "Let's sit on this bench. I've got something *awful* to tell you."

The girls trailed along, rolling their eyes at each other. Tress and her theatricals! "Oh, Mary, it's just terrible," Tress began, sitting on the bench while the rest of them dropped on the grass. "I had a screaming row with my mother last night—on account of you," she said to Mary.

Now Mary snapped to attention. "On account of *me*?" Her astonished eyes took in the fact that there was genuine distress on Tress' face. "Why on account of me?"

"Don't you know there's a lot of gossip about you all over our neighborhood?" Tress asked. While Mary looked blank, Tress went on: "Your hateful old neighbor, Mrs. McDrey, is a bosom buddy of our hateful old neighbor, Mrs. Hazenstad. And Mrs. McDrey has been gossiping all week, all over—helped out by Mrs. Hazenstad,—telling how you went sneaking into your house at six o'clock the other Sunday morning, after leaving the evening before with Andy—and coming back with Andy. They—they've concluded the worst, Mary. I hate to tell you.

"And," Tress went on, "I hate to tell you this too. My Mom says I'm not to be seen with you for a while!"

"What are you saying?" Jodell gasped as Mary felt her face go crimson. "Tress Higgins, what are you talking about now?"

A sheen of tears washed down Tress' cheeks. "You know how my mother is," she cried. "She never believes anything I say; she's always suspicious. She's afraid of gossipy neighbors, she believes the worst of everything, anyhow—and it's just your hard luck, Mary, that I stood up for you and tried to tell her the truth about it. She always thinks I'm lying. So——" Tress stood up, dabbing angrily at her eyes—"I'm so sorry, Mary. You know I'll see you whenever I can. But if I'm caught, my mother has her way of making me regret my disobedience. Oh, Mary, I'm sorry!" Tress dashed from among them, running awkwardly, as though she couldn't see where she was going.

"Well, I'll be darned," Jodell muttered. Barbie reached over and laid her hand on Mary's. "Don't care," she said softly. "You know how hysterical Mrs. Higgins gets. And Tress exaggerates things. It'll blow over, Mary."

Mary sat there, stony and silent. At first she was

stunned and unbelieving. Then she began to get mad
—like mercury crawling up a thermometer.

By the time she had got slowly to her feet, the blood
was pounding in her head and she was thoroughly
angry. "This is unfair!" she cried. "How could those
horrible women make up something so awful out of
something innocent that was just an accident? How
could anyone have such a low mind that she'd think—
ooooh, I'm so furious!"

"Tress shouldn't have told you," Barbie said. "She
likes to stir things up. I don't believe this is half as
bad as she makes out."

"Tress wasn't making this up," Jodell said soberly.
"She was really upset. One thing she is, and that's
loyal. And she had to explain why she can't be with
you, Mary. As she says, her mother is always suspicious
and never believes a thing Tress says. Naturally, that
makes Tress feel there's no percentage in telling the
truth. It's all very stupid, Mary. I'm terribly sorry."

"But it's so unfair!" Mary exploded again. "It isn't
true, it simply isn't true, that we'd deliberately stay
out all night. Andy's always been just—just simply
swell. And people ought to know me. Oh, it's not fair!"

"They don't know you," Jodell reminded her seri-
ously. "It wouldn't be possible, I guess, for a crabby
old lady like Mrs. McDrey, who has never had children of her own, either to understand how a girl of
seventeen feels or to believe anything but the worst

of any teen-agers because of all the hullaba
juvenile delinquency. Without knowing us, a
people think we're all bad."

"Well, she'll have a chance to find out about me,
Mary cried. "Because I'm going over there and tell
her a few things!"

Jodell shook her head. "It won't do any good. It
would only add fuel to the fire. The best thing to do is
just to be above it. I guess everyone gets gossiped
about at some time or other. Especially teen-agers."

Mary went about her housework with a vengeance
that afternoon. *Bang* . . . mean, spying old thing . . .
Thump, thump, fluffing up pillows on the davenport,
I'd like to tell her, I'd like to tell her I don't even
understand a nasty mind like hers . . . *Bang, Bang!*

Her father wouldn't want her to tell off Mrs. Mc-
Drey. He'd say the things Jodell had said. Her father,
with his trust in the Bible as a guide for bringing up
his children, would give her one of the many quotes
that seemed to fortify him as he faced his heavy responsibilities: "This, too, shall pass."

Her father . . . Mary stood suddenly still. A picture
of him arose before her.

He'd sit, when he was home, sometimes just sit,
looking so bone-weary . . . and he'd seem to be thinking deeply. His eyes would blink, as though between
the cement dust and the tiredness in them, they hurt.
He'd sit there in his chair . . . and gradually he'd look

down at his hands. He'd stare at them, occasionally opening and shutting one of them slowly, studying them as though, somehow, he felt there was the answer to all the things he faced in life, as though he felt that, in his big, strong, toiling hands lay his strength.

Oh, Mary thought, he mustn't hear about this. He mustn't worry about me or know I've been hurt. Just because—Mary faced it—just because I cheated a bit, this has happened. And it will hurt him. It might hurt Stevie too.

.... 4

For the first time in her life Mary knew what it was
to be oversensitive, to feel that people were looking
at you and whispering about you behind your back.
Heretofore, she had always been too absorbed in her
busy life; too sure, when she thought about it at all,
of her lack of importance in the general scheme of
things, to believe that she could be very much in the
limelight. In fact, she had consistently avoided the
limelight.

Now, as she started off for school on Thursday
morning, after a night when she thought she couldn't
have slept at all, she kept her head turned so that she
was completely ignoring the old lady's house next
door. Yet, as she hurried away, head in the air, eyes
right, she could almost feel the breeze at her back,
fanned by the swishing of the lace curtains in Mrs.
McDrey's windows. And each house, as Mary prog-
ressed down the street, seemed suddenly all eyes, un-

[53]

friendly, sneering eyes, all peering at her; all the owners of them whispering: That's the Munday girl who stayed out all night with that fellow. She *looks* like a tramp, doesn't she?

Mary's back prickled as though the slings and arrows of spying eyes and vicious tongues were bombarding her from behind. She rushed along, miserable and angry. She had only gone a block or so when she heard a call and whistles behind her—and there, running after her, were Jodell and Barbie. She didn't exactly want to face them this morning. And yet a quick lump rose in her throat at sight of them and their obvious desire to be with her. She waited.

They caught up with her, panting. "Why didn't you wait for us?" Barbie demanded, catching her breath and mopping her brow. And Jodell, with a keen glance at Mary, said, "You needn't snub us, child. We're in your corner, you know. You're still all het up this morning, aren't you?"

"I'm all right," Mary said. She didn't want to talk about it.

"I went over to Jodell's to study last night," Barbie said. "And it got late, so I stayed all night. We haven't had much sleep." She grinned. "Talking till all hours."

Talking . . . about me and my scandal. "Understand, I like Mary, *you* know that," Barbie would say. "And I believe her too. Only I never thought she'd lie to her Dad—well, not exactly lie, but cheat a little, you know what I mean. You never can tell, can you? She'd never have gotten into this mess if she'd minded her father."

"Well, it was foolish of her," Jodell would say, in her outspoken way. "I hate the way everyone is talking about her." Jodell would be stanch: "We've got to stick by her, no matter what anyone says."

Mary shook herself. Her friends, her very best friends. If she couldn't trust them not to talk about her, things were in a sad state indeed. She relaxed and tried to put warmth into her voice, though she felt cold. "Let's hustle," she said. "I want to speak to Mrs. Donner on my term paper. She said five thousand words and I've only got twenty-three hundred and that covers the subject, as far as I'm concerned."

She thought, as they approached the grounds of Central, that quite a few of the kids seemed to pause in their conversation to stare at her—an aware look; not as though they saw-and-yet-didn't-see her, the way people pass each other when they're absorbed in their own conversations and affairs. Maybe she was wrong.

She hoped she was.

She hurried into Home Room 102 and went up to Mrs. Donner, who was talking to a couple of other students. Mary waited till the conversation was finished.

She was crazy about Mrs. Donner. Young, red-haired, rather clever and sassy, Mrs. Donner had a way of looking at you when she talked that made you feel she saw through you with her cool green eyes, but yet she was on your side too. I hope she's on my side, Mary reflected unhappily. In fact, I hope she never hears the other side.

How far and how fast can gossip travel, block by block . . . gossip starting in one neighborhood? Does it travel with the speed of sound, jumping street crossings . . . penetrating, like gamma rays, into buildings . . . buzzing along like an intercom system . . . ?

"Well, hello, Mary," Mrs. Donner turned to her. "Don't tell me now that you studied *all* night. Or was it a heavy date?"

Mary colored. What did she mean by *that*? . . . Behave, Mary Munday, you're as jumpy as a hound dog with fleas.

She conferred briefly with Mrs. Donner before the bell rang. "Just put the meat of the subject down without padding. Remember, I know how much you actually know on the subject. Just do your usual good job. And I hope you get rested up in class today."

Mary turned away quickly. *It ain't funny, McGee.*

That was a wretched day in Mary's life. She felt as though she were skulking down the halls. In class, she couldn't keep her mind on the subject at hand and twice got caught off-guard by questions. She stayed away from her locker at noon, which was where Andy usually came to look for her when he wanted her.

[56]

Maybe he wouldn't even be wanting her today. But she didn't mean to face him anyhow.

Mary Munday, a girl so gossiped about that a mother had forbidden her daughter to be seen with her—Mary Munday.

She and Jodell and Lutie ate lunch out in a far corner of the grounds. There was no danger of meeting Andy right now, for his lunch period was before hers. He only had about five minutes' leeway between classes. It always rushed him when he waited for her between lunch periods.

Mary and Jodell walked home together that afternoon, Mary subdued and dispirited, both of them yawning.

Mary was putting a Swiss steak into the oven when the phone rang soon after she got home. She had summarily ordered Stevie to change his clothes fast and to get out to his grass-cutting job. There had been no overtones of relenting in her voice, so the lawn mower was whirring loudly outside the window as she picked up the phone.

Andy's voice demanded, "Where were you today? I waited so long at your locker that I was late for class."

"Oh——" Mary was momentarily flustered, but pleased. "Why, I just got so busy——"

"Fine deal," Andy growled. "Let me know any time I bore you." She laughed. She was glad to hear his voice. "Oh, silly, of course you don't bore me. I'm sorry I wasn't there."

"Well, I wanted to talk to you," Andy said soberly. And Mary, after a second's pause, said, "Yes?"

"Yeah. Would you think I'm a real chintz, Mary, if I asked that we just stay home and watch TV, or something, tomorrow night? It hurts my pride to ask you. But I had to put out forty-five dollars for the jeep all in one lump sum, borrowing some of it from my Dad—in fact, by the time they got through adding every little item they could, the bill was forty-seven-seventy-five. It took every cent I had and now my dad says I've got to pay him back regularly till I give him the seventeen I borrowed from him."

"Andy," Mary said, "you know me. I don't even think we ought to go out every week and do something that costs money. I always feel guilty about it, I've told you that. I think it'll be swell to watch TV tomorrow night. I'll make some fudge."

"You're a good kid," Andy said. "We'll have us a ball sometime soon, believe me. I wouldn't even dare ask most girls to be such a good sport as you are . . . walking down mountain roads, riding buses, sitting home when I'm broke——"

"Don't be silly," Mary said. "You're awfully stiff-necked about little things, Andy."

"That's the way I am," Andy said, sounding proud of being the way he was. "Well, thanks a million, Mary. I'll see you then."

[58]

How are you, Andy Bremer? How are you going to be when you find out I'm being gossiped about? That Tress' mother has forbidden her daughter—Tress, of all people—to be seen with me? How's your pride going to be then, Andy?

Andy would be all right. Andy, too, was a good sport. A nice kid, her father always said. Everyone said that, Andy's a nice kid. She'd better tell him tomorrow night. It would be a comfort to tell him, to feel that the two of them were facing the world together—the nasty-minded world of the Mrs. McDreys.

But Mary couldn't find the courage to tell Andy that next evening. He seemed in a quiet mood, as he'd been ever since the fiasco of the steak fry. But they sat comfortably together, not talking much, enjoying the Friday-night comedy shows and music on TV, while Dad and Stevie went to the movies.

Somehow, sitting here next to Andy, in the soft light of the one lamp, watching the funny and make-believe world on the screen, trouble seemed minimized, horrid, judging people faraway. Perhaps, by Monday morning, all the dark clouds would be drifted away. Perhaps she, Mary Munday, had been too touchy.

Anyhow, she didn't want to spoil this evening with Andy. And as he left, after her father had come home and was out in the kitchen getting milk for himself and Stevie, Andy kissed her and said, "Nice, wasn't it?" She nodded, and he said, "I'm going to work at the store tomorrow and I'll get paid by seven, so we can go to the show."

Andy worked at one of the neighborhood markets, packing groceries and delivering them when he was not tied up with sports activities. "It's not necessary for us to always be going to the show, Andy," Mary said. But he insisted.

"I've got my pride," he repeated.

However, next morning he called, "My folks want me to go with them up to the cabin tonight. They say I have to help clean it out tomorrow if I expect to be able to take anyone up there this summer. So I'll see you tomorrow night, Mary."

"Swell," Mary said. "We can go to church. There's a special panel group, you know. I'd kind of like to hear it."

Mary watched a couple of television shows that evening with her father and Stevie, and then went reluctantly to her room to do her schoolwork. Never quite enough time for studying, and always so much to do in the spring of the year. But she soon found herself at the window, gazing out at another night of moonlight.

Another lovely, breathless night—a lovely, lonely night. She wondered if Andy, way up there in the family's mountain cabin, was watching the moon and thinking of her, missing her.

She remembered that other night of moonlight

magic. Was it only two weeks ago? She felt again that soft, wonderful feeling, and Andy's tender, firm kiss. So much had happened since then that somehow nothing was quite the same.

The magic and sweetness of life had been tarnished —a little bit—by ugliness. Yet she thought of Andy, of that perfect night, of his feelings for her, and she resolved that she would forget the horrid things, that she would be above the injustice; that she would enjoy Andy's friendship.

She missed him so much tonight.

On Sunday night Andy called for her in the jeep to take her to the church where the young people met on Sunday evenings for either a social hour or, as it was tonight, a discusison group.

Andy seemed strange. He greeted her briefly, without smiling, and they drove almost wordlessly to the church. He looked pensive and unhappy. The freshman-university student who moderated was not too interesting and the discussion dragged. There was only a small group present and the air was muggy-warm, coming in through the open windows.

Mary was bored. More, she was worried about Andy. He hadn't acted the same since the trouble about his car, but he hadn't been like this. Like a first date and both of them shy . . . like a date he perhaps hadn't wanted very much anyhow.

He walked up to the door with her when they arrived back at her house a little before nine. "Come in?" Mary asked but not too hospitably. This reserve business is a game that two can play.

Andy shook his head. He stood there a moment, looking down at her, his face serious. "Do you know," he asked then, his eyes dark in the shadowy moonlight, "that they're talking about us?"

Mary caught her breath. So that's it. So he knows. They're talking about *us*, he said, sharing the blame, sharing the hurt. Just the same, she couldn't bear it for him to know; to know that they were talking about her; that the talk had started about *her*; that it was in *her* neighborhood where the gossip had started; that somehow she would be the one most condemned. She'd never thought about it much before, but now she knew that there is a double standard, and that a girl who stays out all night will be more misjudged than a fellow who stays out all night.

"Yes," Mary said, not looking at him, looking away, her face set.

"My mother is furious," Andy said. "She says if she knew where this started, she'd tell off whoever accused us of—you know. You've got to say that for my mother: once she thinks someone is misjudging her son, she's up in arms. She says she has a lot of faith in me, and that she'll tell anyone who asks that I'm not that kind of a guy."

Mary didn't tell him where the gossip started. That was her fault too, because she didn't get along with her nearest neighbor. *His mother is for him. My Dad is for me too—but he didn't blame Andy. A girl's parents could easily blame the fellow. But Daddy believes in both of us. I wonder what Andy's mother thinks of me. Andy didn't mention that.*

"Well, I'd better go," Andy said. "No telling who's spying on us. It makes me so darned sore. G'night, Mary." He said it softly. Maybe because he didn't want anyone to hear.

He didn't kiss her good night. He gave her a brief smile and was gone.

And Mary cried herself to sleep that night. There was moonlight, the same old moonlight, outside her window. But it was cold and aloof, and it stared scornfully in her window.

Mary was waiting, that Monday afternoon, for her father to come home. She paced nervously during her spasmodic attempts to prepare supper in the kitchen, and kept glancing out the dining-room window where she could see him as he drove in. She had purposely permitted Stevie an extra half-hour to play with some of the boys down the block.

Mary had first meant to throw it at her father—just throw it at him and let him have it—all her anger and hurt and rebellion. But when the car finally appeared and slowed to a halt in the driveway, and her father climbed stiffly out of the car, she knew then that she could not throw anything at him. She would have to be gentle with this gentle man. He would be hurt enough; no need to make it worse.

She had started the day and the week well enough. After a restless night she had awakened that morning with the dispirited feeling that she hadn't the courage to get up and go to school. She felt that Andy's attitude last night had indicated that he was wishing, perhaps subconsciously, that he needn't be involved in this trouble. If it was anyone's fault, it was actually his, yet he didn't want to accept any blame that would smear his name.

She was afraid that Andy might be one of those people who look the other way and retreat when their loyalty is called upon. She didn't want to believe it of him, but he had been so withdrawn and jittery last night.

Mary got up and put on her other new spring outfit —a bouffant, gaily figured, polished cotton skirt and a ruffled yellow blouse she had splurged on at the Blouse Bar. The coffee was fragrant on the morning air and after she had glanced out the window between the fluttering kitchen curtains and had noted the spring sunshine and the newly opened tulips, she suddenly felt better.

In spite of the heaviness in her chest, she knew that she could face the day. So Andy wanted to wash his hands of any gossip? Let him. Never let it be said that Mary Munday was a drag on anyone. Forget it, Mary. Forget him—if that's the way he wants it.

She had stopped expecting spying eyes behind every tree and window curtain. As Jodell said, everybody gets gossiped about at some time or other. *My strength is as the strength of ten,* the poet had comforted such as she, *because my heart is pure.*

It helped that Barbie, Lutie, and Jodell, as though by prearrangement, stopped by for her that morning. They began chattering in lively fashion, as though saying that they'd stand for no foolishness from her. And Mary, smiling, went along with them.

It was a lovely morning. It was good to have friends like Jodell, Lutie, and Barbie. And poor Tress couldn't help it that she had the kind of a mother who listened to gossip and was swayed by it, without trying to find out the true facts. Tress had stopped in the halls of school a couple of times to talk, wistfully, eagerly. Lutie had reported that Tress and her mother did nothing but argue at home.

It seemed, Mary thought suddenly, her steps slowing and her eyes sobering with hidden thought, it seemed awful that she, Mary Munday, who had done nothing wrong, should be made to feel this way . . . not good enough for Tress . . . not decent . . . Not quite good enough for Andy, when it had been Andy's idea to go on a steak fry . . . Andy's car that had broken down.

Oh, stop hiding behind other people! Mary told herself impatiently. *Nobody's to blame. At least I'm not. Forget it, forget it!* She quickened her steps and glanced at the girls to see if they'd noticed her abstraction. They hadn't.

[66]

Mary entered the big door at Central with her head held high and her heart where it belonged, in the center of her chest. She sailed through the first two periods, reciting quite well when called upon. She got to giggling in the hall with Mary Jean Sondergard over a slip of the tongue one of the boys had made in History. "I've been told to discuss women," he said. And then, gulping and blushing furiously, he amended, "I mean *Wilson!*" Inasmuch as he was a very bashful fellow, who hardly spoke to girls at all, he got terribly embarrassed and the class roared with laughter. "Guess that shows where his mind is," Mary Jean giggled.

At noon Mary didn't wait by her locker for Andy. If she didn't wait, she'd never know whether Andy had been there to meet her. If he came and she wasn't there, he'd know that she could get along without him all right—that he needn't be seen with her, if that was the way he wanted it.

Because there was a strong, dusty wind blowing at noon, Mary, Barbie, and Jodell ate in a corner of the lunchroom. Tress, for the first time in days, joined them. They had fun, and Mary's heart lightened till she almost didn't feel it there in her chest any more.

At seventh period she slipped into the gym. Her locker was one of the first and she stopped before it. A group of girls were talking at the other end of the long room, hidden by lockers. Mary recognized the voices of girls she knew.

[67]

"Oh, it's probably true, all right," one of the girls—that would be Edie North—was saying. "My mother heard it pretty directly. And, as Mom says, when a girl hasn't any mother—just an ignorant, laboring-man father—the girl probably can't help running a little wild. Mom says she's sorry for her."

"If she hasn't any mother," another voice broke in—this one Mary couldn't place—"how come she wears those home-madish-looking clothes? Most everything she wears is obviously home-made."

"She makes them herself," Edie North explained. "She's been making her own clothes since eighth grade. I think the family is quite poor. And of course, some of her things aren't so bad—I mean, they're better than I could do."

Now it was Alene Frazier, taking up for her, Mary Munday, in a damning-by-faint-praise sort of way: "Well, I think she's only to be admired if she 'rolls her own.' Otherwise, she probably wouldn't have much to wear, since her father is only a cement worker or something. And he looks as if he's a kindhearted sort of person, though he's probably pretty ignorant."

Mary rushed out of the gym. She didn't care that the door banged behind her. She didn't care that the rushing tears blinded her so that she bumped into someone. She sped for the side basement door at the end of the long hall and rushed out of the building.

She ran most of the way home, crying so hard it was

surprising that she arrived safely, plunging across streets as she did, stumbling on uneven places in the sidewalk, nearly bumping into people, trees, buildings.

She walked the floor of the living room for an hour, beside herself with fury and grief. She felt as if everything in her life had been violently uprooted and blown to bits all around her. All the things that mattered most—and yet the very things about which she seldom thought—her whole background, her whole being, the place where she lived and where all her security lay: these were the things that had been smashed to pieces in a few seconds, smashed by careless, uncaring tongues, smashed because of something that had been entirely an accident.

Her father. Oh, how dared they say such things about her father! Her precious, wonderful, kind, *good* Dad. A laboring man, sure, a man who worked hard, and honestly, long hours, to keep his family together. A man who never asked anything for himself, who just wanted his children to be good and to be happy.

She visualized him, sitting slackly, looking so everlastingly weary, gazing down at his big, gnarled hands, slowly clenching and unclenching his fists; gazing at them with all his worries and all his caring in his tired eyes. A wise man. Oh, how could they call him ignorant?

Mary shook her head furiously and burst into another storm of tears. She had brought this trouble, this terrible misjudgment of her father, on him by her careless, selfish actions.

Her home, her background, reviled by heedless girls with heedless tongues. Her reputation, her clothes— Mary gazed down at the skirt she wore. She had been proud of it. Now she held it up, inspecting it minutely. What showed that it was home-made? The seams, the hem, the cut of it? It was so easy to make; she had chosen good material; she thought it fitted her well. If anything, she had thought that the blouse, purchased at the hole-in-the-wall shop, wasn't as well made as the skirt.

She thought of other clothes she'd made, dresses, blouses, skirts. Home-made clothes. Mrs. Halvorson, her sewing instructor, had particularly commended her on her cleverness with tailoring.

No wonder Andy wasn't anxious to go with her if this was the way people talked about her. Andy . . . the athletic hero, the clean-cut, popular, all-American boy!

She never wanted to see him again as long as she lived.

She had missed the last period of the afternoon. Now she heard Stevie coming in from school. She rushed to the bathroom and was hurrying to bathe her red and swollen eyes when Stevie came pounding up the stairs. He tried the bathroom door, found it locked, and yelled, "Hey, that you, Mary?"

"You can go out and play," Mary called out to him. "You needn't change your clothes if you'll be careful."

"I want to come in!" Stevie shouted.

Mary dried her eyes, and unlocked the door, half turning as she went past him. But there was no slipping past Stevie. As he looked at her his eyes widened. "Hey! Gosh, Mary, what's the matter? Gosh, you look awful! What's the *matter?*"

"It's nothing. I just got mad at school. Go ahead, Steve. Go and play."

"Can I do anything?" Stevie persisted. "Who made you mad?"

"It's all right," Mary said impatiently as she went into her room and closed the door.

She kept the door shut till she heard Stevie leave the house. He had not only changed his clothes—when he didn't have to—but he went quietly down the stairs and remembered not to bang the door. Mary smiled ruefully. Poor little guy. He was really a nice kid . . . even though his father was an ignorant laboring man and his sister a—a tramp who made her own clothes.

Stevie came back to the house once and peered at her, concern in his blue eyes. "You all right, Mary? Want me for anything?"

Mary mustered a smile and assured him that she was all right. That was when she thought to tell him he could play with his gang half an hour longer than usual.

And so she waited for her father to come home.

"Hello there, honey," he said, coming in the door. And then, though she was relatively quiet now and her face was not so swollen and blotched, he, too asked quickly, "Mary dear, what's the matter?"

"Daddy," Mary said, and tried to say it calmly, "I have to talk to you right away, before Stevie comes home."

"Has something happened to Stevie?"

"No. He's down the street playing. Daddy, I hate to greet you this way. And I'll serve you dinner as fast as I can. But first, would you sit down and let me talk to you, please?"

"Why, sure." There was anxiety in her father's eyes. He sat down heavily, always so weary at the end of the day. Mary got him a cup of steaming coffee, and then sat down opposite him, sitting on the edge of a straight chair, her hands clasped tighly in her lap.

"Please hear me out before you say anything," she said. "I know you're going to be awfully disappointed in me, and I hate it for you, but I just have to do what I think is right in this . . ." She saw fear come into his eyes; a parent is always alarmed when he knows something has happened to his child and he doesn't know what. "Daddy, I'm going to quit school."

Jim Munday wrinkled his brow in dismay and confusion. "Quit school, Mary? Why? When? I've always told you that we'll manage college for you, a bright

[72]

girl like you. It was your mother's big dream."

"I'm not talking about college, Daddy. I mean I'm going to quit now. Tomorrow."

"Quit tomorrow? *Why*, Mary?"

"I'd rather not talk about it," Mary said in a small, tight voice. "I know I owe you some explanation but I hope that right now, at least till I can bear to talk about it, you'll just take my word for it that I couldn't—wouldn't go back."

"But, Mary . . ." The man's face had gone pale; his eyes were troubled. "You have to get an education! That's one of the main things I've worked for. So you won't be ignorant like me."

How could he know that he had said the worst possible thing? How could he know that he had rammed head-on into the sorest spot in her heart?

"Daddy!" The tears were threatening to flood again. "Don't talk like that, you *aren't* ignorant! If I'm ever as wise and good as you—and you got the way you are without more than two years of high school. Well, I want to be just like you!"

"What is it, Mary?" he asked gently, not understanding, but knowing only that his Mary must be badly hurt. "You've always talked to me. Tell me now, what happened?"

"I told you I can't talk about it!" Mary was trying, with her rushing words, to crowd back the growing lump in her throat, the pressing tears. "I know I owe you an explanation," she repeated. "It's just—they've been gossiping about me at school—and around the neighborhood. Mrs. McDrey has been telling people about my being out all night with Andy. Talk . . ."

She saw a blaze of rare anger flare into her father's eyes. She saw his fist clench and unclench. "Who's been talking?" he demanded huskily.

"Daddy, I don't want to make you mad at anyone. I didn't want to tell you any of this. You know what you've always said about getting along. I guess, as you always say, 'This, too, shall pass.' Daddy, please let me handle this in my own way. I wouldn't go back to school even if you did tell off Mrs. McDrey and all the rest of them. Right now I won't go back; nothing will make me go back!"

"Mary, you're running away. That won't settle anything. If you stay right here, facing up, this *will* pass. You're a fine girl, Mary. I don't know what anyone could find to gossip about; but we know it isn't true. People know you're a good girl. Just an old lady's gossip . . ."

She could see that he was stilling his own anger for her sake, but he, too, was hurt and worried.

"Daddy, please trust me! I won't go back. I'm sorry, but I won't go back."

He had seldom argued with her. Perhaps it had never been necessary to do so. "Suppose," he said, on a long-drawn-out breath, "suppose you think it over.

Just while you finish out the year. That's only a month."

"No."

"Suppose, then"—he looked down at his hands— "suppose you stay out of classes for a few days, a week, and think it over."

Mary stood up. "I'm going to start looking for a job tomorrow morning. I won't go back to school. If it's running away, that's the way it will have to be."

"Mary, you could transfer to another one."

She shook her head violently, but she couldn't stand his troubled gaze. "Maybe next year I'll go back," not meaning it, just comforting him. She was never going back. "Even if I'd have to take the semester over again, maybe I'd be ready to go back. But not now."

"Well." Her father's shoulders moved with a huge sigh. "I trust you, my dear. I know you'll figure out what's right when you get it thought out. You're young anyhow, younger than most of your class. You've always been so bright . . . Maybe you need a rest. You've always had to work so much harder than other girls. Try a little vacation, Mary."

She left it that way. She'd won the major point. She didn't mean to have any vacation. She meant to work harder than ever, getting a full-time job and keeping house for her father and brother. She'd let them down enough, she didn't mean to let down on the home front too. And she meant never to go back to school.

But she let him hope for now. You have to ease things whenever you can for fathers . . . parents. They can't seem to face life as resolutely as a young person can.

The future stretched out before her, a long, grueling, work-filled expanse. No more school, no friends. No Andy.

She hurried through supper and the dishes, and then kept busy doing little things around the house.

Jodell phoned, demanding, "Where *were* you? We waited fifteen minutes."

"I had to come home early, I was kind of sick," Mary said. She didn't want to explain now or argue any more. Tomorrow she'd ask Jodell to pick up her things from her locker.

In her room she switched on her bedside radio, hoping for something to fill up her thoughts . . . quick.

A woman's voice pulsed throatily about a phony world and make-believe.

Mary switched off her radio, put her head down, and wept.

····6

Mary started out the next morning as soon as she got Stevie off to school. There was a furious desperation within her. She must find a job today. She mustn't think of anything else. She mustn't let down her determination and courage or she would be lost. She mustn't think of her friends, now starting the day in Central.

She mustn't think!

She headed for the State Employment Office. The room she entered was a huge place with all kinds of people milling around and sitting around. If all these people wanted jobs—if they all needed jobs as badly as she, some probably more so—her heart sank.

Uncertainly she approached a desk marked *Receptionist*. A young woman looked up and smiled at her pleasantly. "May I help you?"

This helped already. Someone had time for her, someone wanted to help.

"I—I'm looking for a job," Mary said, ending strong on the last word.

"And what kind of a job?" the young woman asked. "Have you any experience?"

"I just need a job," Mary told her. "I don't have—much experience."

"Well, now, let's go consult Mrs. Bowes," the receptionist said, eying Mary thoughtfully. She led the way between desks and people. "Miss Bowes," she said, stopping before one of the desks, "here is a girl who'd like to talk to you."

Mrs. Bowes was a middle-aged woman and there was kindness in her bright eyes. She said good-by to the girl who was just leaving her desk and then turned to Mary. "Now, what may I do for you?" she smiled.

Mary told her. She needed a job right away. She had thought maybe she'd like to be a receptionist in a doctor's or dentist's office.

The older woman extracted a card from a drawer and prepared to take down information. Name. Address. Age. Schooling. Experience. Mary hurried over the schooling bit. Before this woman's keen eyes she felt she was on shaky ground should she have to explain why she wasn't in school. Mrs. Bowes asked her about typing and shorthand experience.

"I haven't had shorthand," Mary confessed. "But I had typing last semester." She didn't mention that it had been her weakest subject.

[78]

WALK IN THE MOONLIGHT

"And do you know how many words you can do a minute?" Mrs. Bowes prodded.

"I—I don't know. About thirty?" Mary offered hopefully.

Mrs. Bowes said, "Well, now, we'll give you a test to see what you can do."

Another woman gave Mary a typing test. She did a rather poor thirty, making a number of errors, partly because she was so nervous. Mrs. Bowes was still kind. "We'll try to find a place where you don't need shorthand and where your typing isn't important. Jobs like that do come up. There aren't very many receptionist's jobs around, but we'll try. And you say you have no experience in anything. Hmmm. Well, we'll call you, Miss Munday."

"There wouldn't be any place I could apply today?" Mary pleaded.

"Not that we have listed right now," Mrs. Bowes said. "Your age and your lack of experience—but we'll do the very best we can for you."

Mary walked out of the place on wobbly legs and with an empty feeling in the pit of her stomach. She felt so let down she wanted to flop on the curb and cry. She considered briefly boarding a bus and going on downtown, making the rounds from office to office, and applying in person. But she had no courage left to do this.

She took the bus home. Maybe that horrible void in

her middle was hunger. She arrived home and cried and ate lunch.

During the two days that Mary waited for the employment office to call, she feverishly cleaned house. She was learning early a truth that dawns sooner or later on almost everyone: working hard helps when there is a pain in the heart or a problem in the head.

The girls came by after school and tried to reason with her. Jodell had reluctantly, at Mary's insistence, brought home the things from Mary's locker. Tress came with the others and begged Mary to come back to school. "You're making me feel it's all my fault," Tress cried.

"It isn't your fault," Mary said. "This is just something I'm going to do because I'm fed up. Nothing you can say will change my mind, so please don't talk about it."

She had told only Jodell about what she had overheard that day in the gym and Jodell was sworn to secrecy. When she once promised, she kept her word. She might turn a frosty eye upon Edie North and Alene Frazier, who had been participants in the thoughtless discussion that had so hurt her, but they'd be puzzled as to why. Jodell and daisies never tell.

Andy hadn't called. On Tuesday, Jodell reported, "Andy came up to me in the hall after third period today and asked where you were. When I told him you had quit school, he looked as if he were going to cry."

"He won't cry," Mary said stonily.

And he didn't call that night . . . after he knew.

So then Mary knew that he, too, was afraid. Afraid of gossip, afraid of people; afraid he couldn't maintain his reputation as a nice boy, a popular guy, should he be involved in any gossip—gossip about Mary Munday.

It was becoming obvious that she was going to bear the brunt of the whole episode.

Maybe Andy was glad to be rid of her anyhow. Maybe he'd been looking for an excuse. Her home-made clothes, her poor and ignorant background.

Mary's father was very gentle with her. She knew he was watching her, watching and worrying, but he said nothing.

On Wednesday they phoned from Stevie's school, reporting that he had an upset stomach and they were sending him home.

Quit picking on me, Mary told life as she let her pale little brother in the door and then had to rush him to the bathroom where he was thoroughly sick. *What a lousy week. Everything was wrong.*

But then she was ashamed after she put Stevie to bed and was cleaning up. *Sorry for yourself, Mary Munday, when the poor little guy is so miserable.* It always seemed to frighten him so much when he . . . regurgitated. (She tried to put it fastidiously, not feeling too well herself.)

She was kept busy for the next hour or so, trying to

[81]

make Stevie comfortable. When he felt a little better, he became immediately restless, which necessitated firm measures. By suppertime he was all right, but Mary resolutely fed him soup and crackers and made him stay in bed.

"I haven't time to nurse you," she told him severely, in her relief that this was evidently only a temporary upset. "And I wish you'd quit making a pig of yourself."

On Thursday morning she couldn't wait any longer and went to the employment office again. Mrs. Bowes shook her head. "I called the places we have listed. Their jobs are either filled or they want more typing experience. Would you be interested in some other kind of a job?"

"Yes," Mary said. "Yes, I would. What else is there?"

"Well, let me see," Mrs. Bowes reflected, flipping through cards. "Hmmm . . . this one takes quite a bit of typing. This calls for experience . . . You did say you have no experience as a sales clerk, didn't you?"

"I've had no experience in anything," Mary said. "But how do they expect you to start working if they don't let you get experience on the job?"

Mrs. Bowes smiled. "That's a good question. We hear it a dozen times a day. Let me see here—Mary, you wouldn't want to work in a restaurant, would you?"

Out of the frying pan into the frying pan! "Right now," Mary sighed, "I'll try anything."

Mrs. Bowes gave Mary a referral card and directed her to the restaurant where a waitress was wanted. Peering in the windows as she approached the place, Mary thought she wouldn't mind working here. It was a nice restaurant and the girls inside, waiting on the tables, wore attractive yellow uniforms and caps. Tips might be good in a place like this.

The position, the hostess at the cash register informed her superciliously, had just been filled.

But Mary had an idea. She was going out on her own and get a job as a waitress. She started out.

She began with the better places, the larger ones and those uptown. There were no vacancies or else they wanted experienced girls. One man around noontime, when Mary was hot, tired, and discouraged, got her to sit down beside him in the lobby of the place. "You look warm and tired," he said kindly. "Let me get you a Coke." He left and returned with a tall glass. "How old are you, little lady?" he asked.

"Seventeen," Mary told him, slipping her feet slightly out of her shoes and sipping the drink gratefully. But I'm strong. And I'm used to work."

The man was studying her. "Why aren't you in school?" He saw that she didn't want to answer and he went on then. "Listen to me. You're a nice-looking girl. You belong in school, having dates and fun. Do you know what a hard life it is, working in a place like this? If I should give you a job—which I can't, you simply have to have experience—you'd be on your feet for eight hours, rushing almost every moment, carrying heavy orders. I pay my girls well and they earn every cent of it, and the tips besides. During the rush hour they work like dogs. Now be a good girl and go home and forget this waitress kick. I'll bet your mother and father don't want you to quit school and work, for whatever reasons you have in your pretty little head. You look like a girl whose folks care about her. Go back to school, won't you?"

Mary bobbed her head in such a way that he could make what he would of it. He was being nice to her. He didn't seem to think she was a frump. She thought of asking him if he turned down all applicants as tactfully as this. But instead she managed a wavery smile for him and said, "Thanks." Cramming her feet into her pinching shoes, she left the restaurant.

He probably thinks I've gone home, a reformed character. Well, I'm not. I won't. I can't.

So she looked like a girl who belonged in school, having fun and dates. A little girl whose folks . . . She decided she'd have to lie about her age.

She went to several more places and told them she was eighteen. No soap.

As one o'clock approached, she was wandering on Seventeenth Street, lost and empty. She passed hurrying, chattering groups of girls and women, all obviously going from their jobs to lunch. She was again attacked by a feeling of insignificance. If all these assured-acting, smart-looking people had jobs, what chance was there for an inexperienced seventeen-year-old? She stopped in a drugstore to have a malted milk and consider the problem further.

Then, almost ready to quit for the day, she noticed a sign in the window of a small place called Brody's: *Waitress Wanted.* She entered the restaurant, and immediately the rank smell of hot grease assailed her nose, the odor of day-in-and-day-out, month-in-and-month-out, food being fried in heavy grease.

It was a very small place, neither very clean nor very attractive. And the man standing behind the cash register didn't look as though he wanted much of anything that life had to offer him. But the sign had said he wanted a waitress, so Mary approached him.

"I'd like to apply for that job as waitress," Mary said.

The man eyed her sourly. He was a short, scrawny man with crooked, stained teeth and a bored expression in his brown eyes. He gazed at her without visible enthusiasm. "Had any experience?"

"No, but I'm a hard worker."

"How old are you? What's your name?"

"I'm eighteen," Mary said, looking him straight in his dull brown eyes. "My name is Mary Munday."

[85]

"Salary's thirty-five a week. There's tips—usually. My name's Brody. I'm the boss. M'wife, Mame, is here most of the time in the kitchen. I guess *she's* boss. Stelle Larson's the other waitress. She's on days. I'll want you nights. Wait here, I'll get Stelle. She'll stay tomorrow night to show you the ropes."

Mr. Brody sauntered toward the sound and the smell of the kitchen in the rear. He went through a door that closed behind him. Mary glanced about her.

There was a horseshoe-shaped counter in the center of the narrow room. At the front of the counter was the cash register where Mr. Brody evidently officiated. Behind this were the glass cases that contained individual packages of cereals, condiments, buns, a cut pie or two, some cakes, and a pyramid of such canned goods as beans, spaghetti, chili, Spanish rice, and soups. Along either side of the counter were small booths, four to a side. At present there was no one in any of them. A juke box, by the front entrance, stood silent.

Mr. Brody returned, followed by Stelle. At first glance Mary wondered what a woman like Stelle was doing in a place like this. At a distance she looked like class with a capital C. She was a handsome blonde with her hair perfectly coiffed. There was a certain grace to her walk as she followed Mr. Brody. As she came near, however, flaws became apparent. The hair had not always been blonde, at least not this unusual type of blondeness; the face was so heavily made up it was like a mask; and there was a hardness to the eye which suggested that Stelle had been around too much, too long.

Evidently she felt that Mary was out of place here too. Staring out of her hard blue eyes, she said to Mr. Brody, "Well! You really are desperate this time, aren't you? This is the worst job of cradle-snatching you've ever done. How old are you, honey?" she asked Mary.

Mary's dander was up. It would be fun, she thought, to ask *her* how old *she* is! "I'm eighteen!" Mary said aloud, trying to match cold stare for cold stare.

Stelle shrugged. "Could be," she said. "Well, welcome to the Old Manse, honey. I'll give you the dope —and I don't mean Brody."

"That'll do, Stelle," Mr. Brody growled. To Mary he said, "I'll want you for the evening shift, five to twelve, six nights a week. Be here at five tomorrow night. Stelle'll stay on to show you the ropes. Meanwhile get yourself a uniform like Stelle's."

"They're five-ninety-eight at Montgomery Ward," Stelle volunteered. "Might as well get the cheapest, you won't be wanting it long." This crack she seemed to divide equally between Mr. Brody and Mary, her malicious glance including them both.

Mary mumbled a "thank you" and walked out before the boss could change his mind . . . before he asked more questions or went into that "little girl who belongs in school" routine. But he didn't look as though he worried one bit about child labor, as long as the child labored for him.

Thirty-five dollars a week! Her own paycheck! She'd concentrate on that, on the feel of real money in her pocket, and she'd forget everything else—the fact that she was going to work in such a place with such a boss, the fact that her evenings would be taken up and there'd be no more dates for her. Dates? With whom?

This way she could be with Stevie until her father came home. She could do the housework and have supper ready every night before she left for the job.

Yes, this was going to be the best thing, all the way around. She could buy things for her Dad, for Stevie, for the house. She could buy *clothes* for herself.

Mary told her father about her new job that evening. She could tell that he was not happy about her working downtown at night, and she hastened to tell him that Brody's served no liquor. However, her father had apparently decided to let Mary work this thing through her own way and so he said nothing. She realized that somewhere deep inside she had hoped he would object, that he would save her by refusing to let her take this job.

Instead, he remained silent. Who said Jim Munday wasn't a wise man?

Mary suspected that her father thought the more unpleasant the job, the faster she'd tire of the whole thing. She'd have to show him.

She'd have to show the whole world.

She went to bed early, so exhausted that she fell immediately into a deep but troubled sleep, and her dreams filled with strange, unpleasant faceless throngs who didn't seem to think much of Mary Munday.

When Mary arrived a little before five for work the next evening, Mr. Brody led her out to the kitchen to introduce her to his wife, Mame. Neither the kitchen nor Mame were very appetizing. Mrs. Brody was as scrawny as her husband, with a driven, harried eye, and Mary had a momentary feeling of pity for her, thinking that the poor woman's life must be miserable, between her sour husband and the hard-eyed Stelle, plus a life among the pots and pans in this dark, moldy kitchen.

Then Mrs. Brody began to talk and Mary's pity soon died, washed under by the torrent. Never had she been around anyone who could talk a mile a minute like Mame Brody.

"Well, if you say you're eighteen, I guess you know what you're talking about. But you look younger and greener to me. Sometime they'll get Brody for hiring 'em before they're dry behind the ears, but he never listens to me. Oh, well, it'll be on his own head. Stelle'll show you what to do and you'd better get busy right away; we usually got quite a push on Friday nights. I'm washing the dishes tonight till we can get another boy, the last one didn't show up—not a word of warning, just didn't show up. Kids are so irresponsible these days. Know any boy who wants a dish-washing job? You better not stand there; get busy. *Stelle!*"

There were two men eating at the counter and Stelle was waiting on a couple in one of the back booths. "One and one without!" Stelle sang out through the window opening between the lunchroom and the kitchen. Then she came over and began to instruct Mary in "the ropes."

"Here's a pad and pencil for you. You write down everything and don't be afraid to ask questions till you get it right. Customers, even the kind who come in here—or I should say, especially the kind who come in here because I've never known it to fail, the less they've got at home, the more they holler in public— are all fussy, and so's Mame. You'll soon learn to make out. There isn't any way you can please the Brodys, so don't try. Just do the best you can. Now, when you have time, when you first come in, or else before you leave at night, you fill the setups—the paper napkins, toothpicks, sugar bowls, creamers, salt, pepper, all those things."

"Do I wash them beforehand?" Mary asked, and Stelle snorted. "Every day? Heavens, no! You empty and wash them once a week, but you take a damp cloth and polish them where they're dirty—or where they show. We keep the condiments in the glass case and make 'em ask for 'em if they want them. No waste. That's Brody's. After your customers leave, you clear off the dishes—first being sure to pick up the tip, if any—and put them in that tub over there at the back of the counter. Usually there's a boy to wash them, a new one every week or so. Before you leave at night, you wipe down the back counter.

"Now here's the regular menu," Stelle went on. "We serve breakfast any time, because we're near the railroad and in some of the places around here men work on shifts. And we always have these short orders on hand: hamburgers, cold sandwiches, bacon-and, ham-and, sausage-and, fried and cold ham, pork chops, chicken-fried steaks—if they ask for either veal cutlets or chicken-fried steak, you can always say we got it, because they're the same thing around here. Then you get a choice of a couple of specials each day. Like today being Friday, we've got halibut steak and braised tips. Maybe it'll be sauerkraut and hot dogs or pork loin—oiyoy, *what* loin? Mostly we do short orders because if people have enough money to eat a regular meal out, they find someplace better. I hope you don't lose your appetite here, kid, and that glowy skin of yours. But then, you won't be here long. They never are. Don't look so unhappy, you'll be lucky the day they toss you out."

Mary ventured, "Why do you stay here?"

Stelle smoothed one caressing hand down one hip and the other up one side of her coif, in true movie-siren fashion. "They pay me pretty good," she said coolly, "to provide class to the joint. And I get my own way because old Brody don't dare fire me. Mame would've long ago if she could. But he knows what side his crummy bread's buttered on. Say, that's a joke, isn't it? It just come out, just like that—'crummy bread,' get it? Crummy joke, isn't it?

"Now," she continued, "there's a booth of customers come in. Go take the order, kid."

"Couldn't I observe you first?" Mary cried, panic-stricken. "Just this once?"

"Nothing like wading right in," Stelle said, giving her a little push. "Go on now. One more thing, if any man gets smart, clomp down on him hard. It's the only way to keep the geezers in line."

So Mary, in fear and trembling, took her first order. She didn't do too badly. Before the evening was over, she had taken quite a few orders and had mixed things up only slightly. Stelle helped her. Mr. Brody stood behind the cash register and looked glum. And in the kitchen, Mrs. Brody banged pans, sloshed dishwater, and talked all the time—to herself if no one else was around.

That Friday evening, which Mrs. Brody had said would be "quite a push," was not too busy, and the time dragged. Mary looked out the window and saw kids going by—the high school gang, out on the town because it was Friday. At the Denver was a rock'n'roll film. At the Orpheum a big picture. At the Paramount one of the creatures-from-outer-space things. A bevy of pretty girls in frothy formals drifted by with fellows in tuxes . . . Mary remembered a dance one of the smart set held at the Cosmo. Probably it was that group, out seeking fun or a snack. They never even considered Brody's as they sailed by, their voices gay.

And here was Mary Munday, working in Brody's. What was Andy doing tonight? Suddenly she became convinced that he might be going past at any moment. Going past with another girl . . . She grew panicky. She would die if Andy saw her now, a waitress in a place like this. And if he did see her, he'd probably snub her. He'd wish he'd never met her.

Was it, could it be, only three weeks ago tonight that she and Andy had had that perfect evening, when all the world had seemed so magical? She

[94]

thought she must look like Stelle now as she felt her face and her heart go hard and bitter.

Her father was waiting for her when she got home. He looked sleepy but obviously relieved at sight of her. "How did it go?" he asked.

"Pretty good," Mary said lightly. "Not too busy, and I didn't make too many mistakes. You shouldn't have waited, Daddy. I'm a big girl now—earning my own living, you know."

She smiled at him brightly, wanting to reassure him in every way she could. She hoped he'd never decide to visit Brody's, for she had an idea he wouldn't think too highly of it as a setting for his daughter. He, at least, seemed to think she was rather special. The only person who did . . .

She wanted to ask, with great casualness, if there had been any calls. But she didn't. Instead, she asked, "Did you and Stevie go to the show?"

"No," Jim Munday said. "You remember, he went to the school carnival tonight. I went over for a while and then I came home about eight-thirty. When I got here, Andy was just leaving."

"Oh?" Now she was very casual. So much so that she hardly got her voice out at all. "Andy?" (Who's he?)

"Yes. I invited him in and he stayed a little while. When I told him what you're doing, Mary, he looked sick."

"He did, did he? So what is new with him?"

"He didn't say much," her father said. "Seemed to miss you, and to be unhappy. He says he'll call."

"Fine," Mary said. "Now let's get to bed. I've got both the wash and the ironing to do tomorrow, you know."

"We'll hire someone to do it," her father said. "You can't do everything."

"Let me try first," Mary said. "I can space it out during the week now. Everything's going to work out fine," she told him cheerfully.

She went to her room, slipped off her clothes, and got into bed quickly. As tired as she was, she expected to drop off to sleep right away.

She didn't. She lay on her back gazing up into the darkness. The night was very still. And in the silence she listened to her thoughts.

She had no pride left to go on. She was as bad as any of the lovesick girls she had made fun of in times past. She wanted to see Andy terribly. Even though he had deserted her—or at least had showed signs of wanting to desert her—when the first sign of trouble came, still she wanted to see him. Clay feet and all.

She wanted to go back to where she had been three weeks before. A schoolgirl . . . fun . . . no worries . . . dates. Andy.

But she was out of school. She had no friends, she told herself. She had no Andy. She was a waitress in a *joint* (to quote Stelle.) Her reputation was ruined, her future was zero.

Oh, Andy. She wanted to feel the comfort of his arms. The hot tears rolled down both sides of her face as she lay there, gazing into the darkness.

....8

The next few weeks were filled with days and nights of great emptiness for Mary, the worst through which she had lived. She thought back to the time of her mother's death and remembered her first lonely grief. But then she had been a child. She remembered how kind so many people had been to her, especially her father, who must have been heartbroken himself. Her favorite aunt had come from her home in the East to care for the ten-year-old girl and the new baby, Stevie, and had stayed several months. Neighbors, friends, the minister, everyone had been kind.

Now Mary felt so alone with the problems of her own making. And there was no color but dull gray or ugly black in the world through which she moved right now. Mornings and noons, she was home alone while others her age, her friends, were together in school. Evenings, when others were either home or dating, she was working. And for companions she had a pickle-faced boss, a crabby, yakking Mame, and occasionally the hard-eyed Stelle.

Before, she had wished that one could be given the power to foresee the future. And now she knew that this would never do. Had she been able, a number of weeks back, to know that all this trouble was coming into her life, what would she have done? What *could* she have done? She still felt she had taken the only step possible.

Well, all she could do was to grit her teeth and live day by day, always with the hope that tomorrow would be better.

Though she was often sunk in such depths of despair, everything was not hopelessly lost. There was her father, loving her, believing in her. Sometimes she thought that his searching, tender gaze only made things harder to bear, but she also realized that she needed his strength behind her. He was the greatest strength she had. And there was Stevie, who needed her.

Also, Jodell, Barbie, and Lutie would not give her up, even though she tried to convince them that she was no longer a part of their world. "Don't be silly," they said.

And Jodell added, "Even though you're such a dope, we like you." The girls came by after school and visited with her, they spent as much time as they could with her on Saturdays and Sundays.

Her father reported that Mrs. Donner came to the house one evening, asking for her. But after a talk with Jim Munday, Mrs. Donner went away again, leaving no message. *She was probably thoroughly disgusted with me. So ends another beautiful friendship,* Mary thought bleakly.

Came the final week of school and the night of Central's graduation exercises, and Mary was waiting on customers in Brody's restaurant. She wouldn't have been graduating anyhow, but several of her friends were, including Lutie. Mary went shopping and splurged, ostentatiously, with her own money, buying for Lutie an adorable pair of polka-dot shortie nylon pajamas.

She heard that Andy had got a good job with the Forestry Service and was going to Wyoming. He didn't come near her or call to say good-by, and she told herself harshly that she was glad, that she wouldn't have talked to him anyhow.

And so Andy was gone.

The heat of summer came on, and between the long hours of work at home and at Brody's, Mary lost her appetite. The restaurant's greasy smell, the handling and serving of food, and Mame's none-too-clean cooking habits added to her own general unhappiness. When she looked in the mirror, she saw that her face was thin, her eyes dull and tired. *Mirror, mirror, on the wall, who's the fairest of them all?* Not Mary Munday, that's for sure. She didn't like what she saw in the mirror, so she tried not to look any more than she had to.

She caught her father sometimes staring off into space, and she would not let herself see the trouble in his face.

Gradually, in spite of herself, she began to develop a slowly awakening interest in the café. She would have denied it, but there it was. In the first place, she came to realize that Mr. Brody's crusty exterior covered up the fact that he was a man of fundamental kindness, at least toward her. She understood that his morose ways were due in part to the fact that he had built up a wall of resistance and a deafness against his wife's incessant babbling. Mary was learning to try to ignore Mame too.

As for Stelle, the flip and brittle line she had was at least weirdly fascinating . . . sometimes. Mary decided, watching Stelle in action, that her advice was meant for others and not for herself, for Stelle seemed to encourage men to "get smart." And the only ones she "clomped down on" were those she decided were "characters."

On the other hand, Mary decided that her youth must stick out like a sore thumb. For never once, in all the time she worked for Brody's, did she have to "clomp down" on a man. Some men were gruff or oblivious, but most men, even the roughest-looking ones, treated her with respect or even a sort of protectiveness. When her father questioned her anxiously about this, she told him, "I must look like a baby-face, they never act toward me as they do toward Stelle. In fact, they treat me like a little girl."

"You look and act," her father said proudly, "like a nice girl. And you usually get back what you give in this world."

And the customers who drifted in and out began to come to life and assumed personalities instead of being vague shapes coming and going, as they had seemed at first.

There was little old Mr. Sippes. He was a shabby, round little man who came in each evening, his paper under his arm and a smile always lighting his pudgy face. His voice was chipper and he loved to talk. Mary was sure, judging by his seedy clothes and the sparseness of his fare, that he must be very poor, but he was always cheerful. He'd read her—or anyone who'd listen—items from the paper and then he'd philosophize about them. He told her he was a salesman for a photography firm and Mary decided it must not be a very lucrative business. She imagined that whatever sales the poor little man made must be because people responded to his interest in them. He was full of stories about his "clientele" and gave the impression that even, without pay, he'd make the door-to-door calls because he "enjoyed meeting the public."

"People are more fun than anything," Mary said carelessly at first, just to answer something. "They are, you know," he said happily. "Each day I get something friendly from the folks I deal with."

She was sorry for her indifference and began to listen to him, and, in doing so, enjoyed it. After all, he had a kind of contentment within himself that she didn't have.

Then there were three older-than-middle-age women, the kind who live in dreary, run-down hotels. Their eyes were feverish with a desire for any bit of excitement, their voices shrill with the need for self-expression. They wore frumpy dresses of a past era, and they tried to talk as though they belonged in this era and as though someone cared.

Ettie Berryhill, Philura Bangs, and Binnie McElfridge. They came fluttering in at dinnertime, their eyes darting about avidly. They ordered meagerly and then huddled over their food, their heads together, reminding Mary of scrawny hens, clucking and scratching in the dust.

They talked to her eagerly, clamoring for her young attention. They touched her clothes, their eyes drinking in her youth. "Dearie, that's how I like your hair best," one would say, and then they'd discuss it, pro and con, as though they all shared her. Mary came to understand that they had to talk about something, had to worry about every detail, savoring every morsel.

Mary saw them strolling the streets of the lower part of town on these humid evenings, and she thought how terrible it was that these poor old creatures should be so alone and unwanted. Out in east Denver . . . or west, south or north . . . there were parks and flowers blooming and the shade of big trees. Here, where these women lived and moved and had all their being, there were only the hot pavements and blackened old buildings, long ago fallen into desuetude (Mary had fallen in love with this word in her English class).

And once Binnie McElfridge phoned to Mr. Brody that she was ill, and asked if Mary could bring some supper to the hotel room. So Mary went, carrying the soup, tea, and rolls which Mame had sputtered weren't worth the trip. "Okay," Mr. Brody said to Mary, "add a couple of them fresh breakfast rolls and a can of sliced peaches. That'll make it worth the trip. But don't charge her," he said *sotto voice*, grinning out of one corner of his mouth. He won Mary's brightest smile.

Fearsomely Mary climbed steep, narrow steps in the dark-halled, smelly little hotel, tapped on the door of 312, and Miss McElfridge's quavering voice called, "Come in!"

The small, dark, stifling room that Mary entered was

so cluttered that she could hardly make her way from the door to the bed where Binnie McElfridge, sallow and gaunt against the pillow, was obviously decked in her best, in Mary's honor, an ancient, faded pink negligée.

Binnie clutched at her with hot hands. "Oh, you dear, sweet child," she whispered hoarsely. "How nice to see you! Sit down by me a moment. I know that horrible woman in Brody's kitchen will be yelling if you don't hurry back—but please, dear, just sit here beside me for a little, will you? I've felt so alone. Ettie and Philura would do anything, just anything, for me. They're all I have in the world. But after all"—she went off into a fit of coughing—"they do have their own problems. Poor things." She lowered her husky voice confidentially. "Have you noticed how Philura's failing lately? You see, they're both *much* older than I am. But, here, let me look at you, my dear. You *are* the prettiest thing—and so sweet. You take me back to when I was your age. I wasn't bad-looking in my time."

Though she looked ill and feverish, and now was coughing with every word, the woman patted her hair and her faded green eyes almost sparkled. Her hair, frizzy and nondescript from many cheap permanents, always hung girlishly in a long bob and had—even now—a tiny velvet bow or two pinned perkily in it.

"I must go," Mary said, smiling warmly at the poor soul. "We're quite busy tonight."

"Oh, I know." Miss McElfridge sank back despondently on her pillow. "I did want to see you. I could have asked one of the girls to bring up some food, but I wanted *you*. Couldn't you just stay one more moment and see some of my treasures, dear? Over there, for instance, that's an heirloom, a clock nearly a hundred years old. And those pictures there, there's my mother and father and my sister that died. All dead. . . . That scarf hanging over that chair was sent me by my boy friend from Paris during the First World War. I was going to marry him but . . ."

"Oh, was he killed?" Mary murmured sympathetically.

"No. He went away . . ." Her voice trailed off.

Mary knew. She could see the shame in Miss McElfridge's eyes. Mary, too, had been walked out on. "You look miserable," she said. "You mustn't talk any more now. Look, I'll bring you your supper tomorrow night. And I tell you what—I'm going to make some good, rich soup at home and I'll come up with some before I go to work!"

"Oh, would you really, dear? I'd love that!" Binnie's cheeks were mottled red, both from fever and from pleasure.

Mary took her the soup the next afternoon and was

received with gratitude, but she was frightened by the look of her patient. After coaxing some of the soup down, she called the doctor, whose number the sick woman whispered to her.

At supper time Philura and Ettie came into Brody's to tell Mary that Binnie had been taken to the hospital.

It was two weeks before Binnie was back, coming into the restaurant, gaunt and ghastly and still coughing—but happy to see Mary and still avid for any scrap of excitement life threw her way.

There was a couple who came into Brody's with their two little boys. "Transients," Stelle said, her lips curling. To Mary they were a worry. The man told her he was in Denver "looking for new business opportunities." But even a teen-ager could figure out the situation.

He was a fellow who talked brashly, his words over-fast and over-confident, while his shifty eyes and the shoddiness of his cheap, loud clothing betrayed a glaring down-and-outness. Mary suspected that "business opportunities" were scarce for him, that he had not been able to hold onto his "positions" in the past, and that he was growing more and more desperate, trying to find someone who would appreciate his peculiar talents and give him a good opportunity, before he finally knuckled under, either to a pick-and-shovel job . . . or to some shady enterprise. The fear in the eyes of his thin little wife, her apologies and loyal

[107]

explanations for him, would have revealed all this in any case. Most of all, Mary was concerned about the two pale little boys who so obviously needed a home and a pick-and-shovel father. Mary found ways to talk Mame into piling the plates higher for this family.

And then one day the family didn't come, nor the next day, nor any more. The anxiety that Mary felt stayed with her for a long time.

Mary learned to sing out: "Baste two!" or, "Two in the water!" or, "One without!" She learned to watch her regular customers' little idiosyncrasies; for instance, Tony Grazzini, the railroad man, who, being left-handed, wanted his coffee to the left of his plate. Mary remembered to cater to these habits. She learned how to keep pretty much out of the way of Mame's flailing tongue, and how to help protect Mr. Brody from his wife's wrath.

The Brodys had a hard time finding a boy who would wash dishes "for peanuts," as Stelle said, and who would also endure Mame Brody. One evening a sixteen-year-old swaggered in, indifferently accepted the job, carelessly gathered and stashed a few piles of dishes, broke a couple of them, and then tossed off his apron and swaggered out to the tune of Mame's furious threats.

So Mrs. Brody continued to slosh dishwater and bang dishes and rant.

Finally another boy was hired for the dishwashing

job. His name was Joe and he was a nondescript fellow of about fifteen. He was furtive-eyed and sallow-complexioned and his Adam's apple bobbed and galloped in a way that fascinated Mary. He did not look or act very bright, but then, as Stelle said to Mr. Brody, "Whadya expect for this job, an electronics engineer?"

Mary helped Joe all she could. He certainly looked like a fellow who needed help. When he didn't clear away dishes fast enough, or didn't seem to see work that had to be done, she found little ways of tipping him off and assisting him. He immediately adored her. He told her that he lived with an older brother who was "mean" to him, that his mother was dead and he didn't know where his father was.

And when, after a couple of weeks of Joe's slapdash dishwashing and dish-breaking, two police officers came looking for him, Mary was stricken. She tried to protect him. She didn't doubt that he could have stolen the hub caps. At least she knew that no great moral qualms would have deterred poor Joe. But she couldn't endure the sight of his sickly pallor and his frantically bucking Adam's apple as he denied the officers' charges.

She pleaded with the kinder-looking of the two officers. "Couldn't I help him . . . sort of be responsible for him? He could pay for the hub caps out of the money he earns here. And I could maybe take him

[109]

home to my father, who is a wonderful man. Or perhaps Mr. Brody . . ."

She glanced hopefully at Mr. Brody, who had already indicated his readiness to please Mary. But Mr. Brody was gazing straight ahead and she saw that there was no help there. He might have a few well-concealed good impulses, but not enough to stick his neck out very far.

"Don't you worry about Joe here," the officer said, a cynical sort of tolerance in his eyes and voice. "Denver is just Joe's home-away-from-home. He's spent more time out on the Hill than he has any place else. The fellows are lonesome for you, Joe. And I'll bet you'll be glad to get back, won't you? Bed and board and movies . . ."

Joe didn't answer but started to move along in a hang-dog way, propelled by the other officer. He turned sad eyes on Mary, a sort of plea for forgiveness in his gaze.

Mary cried when she told her father that night. "It's as though he's never had a chance from the very first. Oh, it isn't fair!"

"There are lots of kids who never have a chance." Her father sighed. "When you think of youngsters brought up in the slums, or perhaps not in the slums, without a mother and father, like this boy—no real home with anyone who cares or treats them well—

And there's a lot of temptation for any boy these days . . ."

She knew he was thinking about Stevie as he said this. She thought of Stevie too. Could he ever become like Joe? Mary shuddered, turned away from the idea, turned back to it.

She and her father were having a difficult time with Stevie this summer. Now that vacation had started and he had time on his hands, except for a couple of lawn jobs and helping Mary, Stevie showed every indication of wanting to run wild.

He was intractable when he and Mary were home alone. And though he moved when his father spoke, it was done sullenly much of the time. Though Joe Munday had never laid a hand on either of his children—"looks to me as if the idea is to make kids *want* to cooperate," he always said, "and you don't make people want to do things without reasoning it out"—Mary thought he had been sorely tempted a couple of times lately when Stevie had been at his defiant worst.

Stevie and Mrs. McDrey had a hassle every day or two. A man up the street came to complain that Stevie continued to ride his bike over his lawn, even though he had been asked not to. One of the neighbors whose lawn Stevie was supposed to keep in shape complained that the boy was quite literally cutting corners on the job. And all the time Stevie was cranky and impudent

. . . or loitering elsewhere when he was supposed to be home.

"Daddy," Mary said now, "Steve will be all right. I know that right now it must seem to you that your two children aren't living up to what you expected of them. But we'll come through all right, both of us. We couldn't help it, with a father like you."

....9

It was a rainy night and chilly for the first of July. Mary watched the streaks of rain streaming down the windows of Brody's. The neon sign across the street was reflected in crazy, distorted rivulets on the windowpanes. There were few customers and they had scuttled in, hugging themselves, for not many had thought to start out with raincoats or umbrellas.

A man entered and seated himself in a back booth. Mary, taking another order, didn't notice him at first. When she did, she walked over and asked, "May I have your order, sir?"

The fellow's dark head was bowed over the paper he was reading, but when he looked up she recognized him. His name was . . . well, she'd know it when she had time to think. He, too, attended Central.

He was a very dark young fellow with curly, close-cropped hair, brown eyes. He was dressed in grease-stained white coveralls.

[113]

As he looked at her, he smiled. "Hey!" he said. "You're Mary Munday!"

It was flattering that he immediately recalled her name when she couldn't think of his. His next question would be, of course, "What are you doing here?"

She remembered things about him now. She had a feeling . . . B.W. Yes, somehow he was a Big Wheel. His eyes were almost black, very striking. He was tall and broad-shouldered, taller than Andy, but somehow she couldn't place him among the athletes. He was very good-looking. Mike . . . Mike?

"I'm Mike Aldo," he told her obligingly. "Gee, it's nice to see you. Nasty night, isn't it? I was going up to Central City tonight, but since it got so stormy, I decided to stay down here and work."

Central City was a restored mining town in the mountains west of Denver where, each summer, an opera and a play were given and people came from all over the country to take part and to make Central City their summer home.

She asked him, "Are you working downtown someplace?"

"Yes," he said. "I'm planning to be an aeronautical engineer, and I'm now acquiring experience as a mechanic's helper in a garage. My Dad thought I ought to work for him this summer, but I want to be on my own and get started as fast as I can. This your summer job?"

"Yes," Mary said hastily. She was recalling other

things about him now. The name Aldo, an Italian name, was well known in Denver because of the large art store run by Mike's father, who was supposed to be the leading local authority in such matters. Mike was a Big Wheel at school, all right, where, in spite of his athletic build, he was known for his mental prowess and also for his independent ways. He had a pretty and popular sister, Joyce, Joyce Aldo.

Now Mary came back to her duties. "Well, what can I do for you?" she asked, putting the menu down before him. She wanted to say, Why do *you* eat in a place like this? But of course she didn't. He evidently worked someplace nearby. She was glad he showed no surprise at finding her there. He evidently thought she was "on her own" too.

Well, she was, wasn't she?

"Gosh, I don't know what I want," Mike said. "What's good?"

She leaned close and dimpled at him: "Nothing."

He chuckled. "Make it a bowl of soup and a piece of banana cream pie. If this be ptomaine, make the most of it."

She brought his soup and he said, "You aren't busy. Sit down and talk to me, won't you? Gee, I'm glad to find you here."

"Can't sit down," she told him. "The Brodys don't encourage the help to associate with the customers. We 'know our place.'"

But she stood by the table, wanting to talk to him.

She hadn't really known him to speak to, but he seemed to remember her. She was feeling lonesome and he was nice.

"You don't know it," he said, "but I've admired you from afar for a long time. I've considered asking you for a date, but you go sailing along with your cute little head in the air and a certain set to your pretty jaw, and you scare men off."

Nothing, absolutely nothing, that anyone had said to her this whole wretched summer set her up so much. Part of the grief of the past weeks was washed away with these words—just as the grime on the windows of Brody's restaurant was being washed down by the pouring rain.

"*My* head in the air?" she gasped, blushing. "You must mean two other gals. I don't know what I've got that would make me hold my head up so high. You're the Big Wheel, you know. And you're handing me a line."

And she liked it! It was wonderful to know that someone, someone like Mike Aldo, thought she had pride.

"You mean," Mike grinned, "that if I'd ask you for a date I wouldn't get the brush-off?"

"One never knows till one tries, does one?" she asked demurely. "Excuse me, please, there are some more customers."

"Hey!" Mike called when she had brought orders

to the two men in another booth. He tossed his head peremptorily. "Come here, will you? I need service!"

She went slowly. And if Mr. Brody, glowering behind the cash register, thought she wasn't alert enough for this highhanded customer, let him. She felt suddenly quite good. Independent.

"Will you bring me my pie, please?" Mike Aldo demanded, a little louder than necessary, for Mr. Brody's ears. "I must get back to work." There was a grin in his eyes for her.

When she had brought the dispirited-looking piece of pie and set it down before him, he said in a lower voice, "What time do you go home? I'll wait."

"Oh," she said, "it's late. You wouldn't be working that long." She was backing away from this. She didn't want any Central interests. Nor any dates with this kind of a fellow, the kind who could hurt her. Mike Aldo looked like the sort you didn't take lightly.

"I'll wait," he said firmly. "What time?"

"After midnight," she said just as firmly. "Please don't wait. I'm always tired and in a hurry to get home."

"Fine," he said. "The better to get you there faster, my dear, in my car."

"No," she said, sort of desperately. "Not tonight."

"See what I told you? You're a real snob. Well, I don't discourage easily, once I've made up my mind. Now that I've found you and you're close to where I work, it obviously was meant to be. I'll be outside at midnight."

She didn't want him to be there, but he was, waiting at the curb in his low-slung Mercury convertible. He was danger. Danger of another hurt, danger of becoming entangled again in things connected with Central.

Her girl friends were, of course, from school, but they were friends, loyal friends. They had stopped arguing with her about her decision because she had asked them to. She had had a date or two, to go to the church Sunday evenings, with Herbie Cates, who also went to Central. But he was a neighbor and did not count. This fellow did.

She pretended to be as tired as she had prophesied and was very quiet. Mike Aldo drove fast, as she knew he would, but expertly, weaving in and out of the late Saturday-night traffic. She noticed that his hands on the wheel were strong and yet relaxed. He drove as though he'd been born behind the wheel. His silence matched hers, his dark eyes steady on the road ahead.

She was nervous, being with him.

"I like your car," she said, finally making small talk. "It rides well."

"I like her myself," he said. He laid one hand on the door by his side and patted it tenderly. "She's a good girl. I've made her that way. Hear that purr? That's because she likes me too. She just responds to me like—well, she's got more response than certain girls I could name!"

Mary gazed straight ahead, saying nothing. Brash, this one. He went on talking about his car: "Maybe you notice that she's got dignity instead of chrome. I don't like these chrome jobs. And that goes for women too. This gal has straight pipes, a planed-down head, and can she go! Want to find out?"

"No thanks," Mary said hastily. "I can tell just by looking at it—at her—and you—that she can go all right."

He chuckled softly. "I've been driving since I was fourteen," he said. "And I've never had an accident, nor even a traffic ticket. I'm an expert driver."

"I'll bet you are," Mary murmured.

"Well, I am!"

"I'm sure of it," Mary assured him. She couldn't help smiling. "And so modest about it all."

He laughed again, and the speedometer edged up a bit higher. Mary sat back and prepared to silence herself.

He stopped before her house. Though she hadn't told him where she lived, he seemed to know. "How about tomorrow night?"

"Oh, oh no," she said. "I'm—busy."

"You don't work Sundays, do you?"

"No, but I—I go to church."

"I've been known to go to church," he said, smiling a little. "Do you have a date?"

"Well, I promised to go with—with my gang."

"What time is church?" he demanded.

"Look," Mary said. She wanted to sound severe but she was afraid it came out pleading. "You don't know me. I'm just a girl who's a waitress in Brody's. I don't——"

"I'm just a guy who's a mechanic's helper in Roadman's," he retorted. "We're a couple of Seventeenth Street serfs. So we ought to stick together. What's the matter with you? Are you trying to give me the brush-off?"

"I'll tell you what's the matter," she said. "I don't intend to have dates this summer. I'm—I'm off men."

He threw back his head and laughed till she was afraid he'd wake the neighbors, Mrs. McDrey for instance. "Hush," she said. "Please stop!"

He stopped abruptly. "I'll be here at seven tomorrow night," he said, starting the motor.

"No," Mary said.

"Yes," he said and drove off.

Well, heck with him. She'd show him.

She showed him. She was ready at seven the next night, wearing a new scooped-neck yellow sheath with an obi sash and bow. She had bought it last Saturday. It was a delicate yellow, and she loved it.

Before this date with Mike there had been some neighborhood excitement.

Mary, taking down some dry clothing from the clothesline early that afternoon, happened to glance toward Mrs. McDrey's house, which she never did intentionally.

At first she thought perhaps a line of Mrs. McDrey's own washing had broken and fallen to the ground. There appeared to be a bundle of clothing in a heap on the other side of the fence. Mary thought maliciously that maybe the old gal would be kept busy redoing her own bedraggled pieces that she wouldn't have time to be spying on her.

But something made her pause, look closer, and then move slowly over to the fence. And then she heard a moan.

Mrs. McDrey lay on the ground, her face distorted, her hand clutched to her breast. She was moaning and gasping for breath.

Mary raced to the house, shouting for her father, who came hurrying up from the basement. Mary led him to the fence and through the gate.

The old woman opened her eyes, which were full of fear and pain and, as she became aware of them, also relief. She seemed to be trying to move her lips, but only a moan escaped. Mary dashed to a nearby lawn chair and, taking a pillow from it, put it gently under Mrs. McDrey's head.

"I'll call the police ambulance," Jim Munday said. "Don't be frightened. They'll be here right away. Don't move her any more, Mary."

While her father was gone, Mary didn't know what

to do. The only thing that occurred to her was to smooth back Mrs. McDrey's hair from around her face and to pat the withered cheek. Mary's hands were trembling.

The ambulance came almost immediately, with siren wailing. The attendants lifted the slight form carefully onto the stretcher and took her away.

Mary thought to say, though she didn't know whether Mrs. McDrey could hear her, "We'll look after your house and yard till you get back."

Her father said, "That was nice of you, Mary. If she heard you, it must have comforted her. We all have to depend on others sooner or later, I guess. She'll realize now that she's lucky to have a girl like you for a neighbor."

"I almost told her off just yesterday," Mary said. "She was yelling at Stevie because she said someone had been reaching through the fence, swiping her rhubarb."

"Which Stevie has probably been doing." Jim Munday sighed. "He's possessed this summer."

"Well, she does goad him," Mary said. "Anyhow, I'm glad I didn't say anything."

"Remember the little verse your mother used to tell you, Mary?

" 'Boys flying kites haul in their white-winged birds.
You can't do that when you're flying words.

Thoughts unexpressed may sometimes fall back
    dead—
But God Himself can't kill them once they're
    said.' "

"I remember," Mary said. "It would be well if a lot of people kept that in mind."

She went about her work the rest of the day, seeing before her the pain-racked and frightened eyes of Mrs. McDrey; remembering how tiny and twisted and helpless, like a discarded heap of old clothes, her body had seemed as the men lifted it—though how strong had been that tongue. She felt very sorry for the poor woman now.

They called the hospital later in the day and found that Mrs. McDrey had suffered a stroke. Jim Munday, entering the old lady's unlocked house, found a card above the telephone in the hall, listing the name of her doctor. The doctor, contacted, said that Mrs. Mc-Drey had a sister living in New Hampshire. This address, too, was listed on the phone memo, and Jim Munday wired her.

"Gosh," said Stevie, asked to water the lawn and flowers in the next yard, "it gives me the creeps to be over there, like she might come any moment and drive me off."

"She can't," Mary assured him. "If you'd seen her, you'd know that she'll be lucky if she ever comes back here. It's kind of funny, isn't it, how now she needs you to be in her yard?"

"I still don't like it," Stevie grumbled. "When she does get home, she'll probably say I ruined everything."

"Stout heart, chappie," Mary said. "You're being a good Scout all over the place—all over the McDrey place."

Mike and Mary drove to the church that night for the supper and the discussion group. Mike was quietly pleasant but Mary was flustered. Somehow he didn't look as though he *belonged* in this group of her friends. He was so—so *spectacular*. She saw the surprised glances when they walked in. She had told Lutie, the only one of her group who belonged to this church. And when Lutie, sitting with her own date, looked back and saw Mike and Mary, up went her eyebrows and she formed a whistle with her lips.

After the meeting, when they had got back to the car, Mike said, "It's such a swell night, let's drive a little—unless you have someplace definite you'd like to go."

"I have to go home," Mary said. "I have a lot of work ahead of me tomorrow."

"I know you have to go home," he said. "And I know you have a lot of work to do tomorrow. I've a lot to do myself. I didn't ask you to drive to Vegas. I said let's take a little ride, okay?"

"Okay," Mary said. Bossy, that's what he was.

It was another night of moonlight, but it didn't do a thing for her. She didn't intend to let it do anything for her—or to her. There was a cooling breeze now, though the day had been hot.

He began to talk. About himself. His voice was a low, pleasant burr, sort of an accompaniment to the car's purr. Burr, purr. Mary only half listened at first, bemused and resisting as she was. "I plan to go into aeronautical engineering," he said. "You know, designing and testing aircraft. I mean to get into field testing. Such things as—oh, skin temperature in rocket flights, stuff like that, you know."

"No, I don't know," Mary said, suddenly interested. "Tell me about it. It sounds exciting."

So he began to tell her: how he had started, as a small boy, constructing airplanes, till he had a room full of them and his collection had overflowed into the garage. He had always enjoyed taking cars apart and putting them together again—as he was doing now at the Roadman garage for more experience. And, after this next year, his last year of high school, he meant to go to California Tech.

"You're all set, aren't you?" Mary asked admiringly. "It must be wonderful to have something you're all

WALK IN THE MOONLIGHT

keyed up about. And to know what you're going to do with your whole future."

"Yes, I guess I am lucky. Ever since I was a kid I've had just one goal in mind. And never time enough to do all the things I want to do."

"I wish," Mary said, "that my little brother Stevie had some sort of aim like that. We—my Dad and I— worry about him. He seems at loose ends this summer, with no particular interest in anything except playing ball—and getting into mischief."

"Has he ever made model planes or boats?"

"Oh, I think he got a car once for a gift and put it together."

"I'd like to meet him," Mike said. "Perhaps I could get him interested. Most kids like it once they get started. A fellow told me that in the Air Corps you can tell which guys had monkeyed with model planes when they were kids; they are the ones who have the savvy when it comes to flying."

"I imagine," Mary said, "that my brother would like to meet you."

"Well, we'll have to get together. Maybe he doesn't have any aptitude that way at all. But if he does, I'd sure like to get him started. I never had a kid brother, and I always wished I did. I've got Joyce—she's my sis, you know—and I'm crazy about her. Do you know her? I think she's a peach, besides being darned good-looking, which you'll admit. We've always been pals.

We're just a year apart. When she was thirteen, she lost interest in making planes and stuff, though we still work on cars together. . . . Now," he said, "I've talked about myself the whole time. You're a good listener, Mary. Now tell me about you."

"I work in Brody's," Mary said. "Not because that's my life's ambition. And otherwise I keep house for my Dad and my brother."

"Yes, I knew that your mother is dead," Mike said. "I've asked questions about you, believe it or not, because I've always had my eye on you. As I said last night, I never got around to asking you for a date, but now I know that we were meant to meet."

So you've asked questions, Mike Aldo. So how much have you found out? You undoubtedly know the scoop about Mary Munday, whose father is an ignorant cement worker, a girl who makes her own clothes and who stays out all night, a girl whom men love and leave. So what does it matter?

"You're a senior this year too, aren't you?" Mike asked. "I'm a year behind because my Dad took us to Europe for a year. He figured that it was part of our education. It's funny you and I never happened to have any classes together. Of course, I went to Smiley Junior High and you must have attended Morey, judging by where you live. I guess I've taken all the science and math I could get—shop and things like that. And naturally you've been interested in other things. What's your major?"

"Oh, English," Mary said. "I—I've always thought I might want to be an airline stewardess."

She didn't tell him she had left school. For good. There was no need right now. Probably there'd never be any need to discuss it with him. It would take a lot of explaining to a guy with such singleness of purpose. Well, she wasn't called upon to explain.

"Swell," he said. "I'll fly 'em and you hostess 'em."

"I never figured," Mary said, "to be a hostess on a jet, thank you just the same."

He laughed. And he took her home. At her door he said, "Good night. I'll call you. And I'll be eating at Brody's."

He gave her a big grin and was gone, running down the walk.

Moonlight, go away. He hadn't tried to kiss her. She hadn't wanted him to. She didn't want anybody's kisses. She was just surprised, that's all. He looked like the kind who works fast.

Moonlight, stay 'way from my door!

....10

That next week Mike Aldo managed to eat in Brody's about as often as mealtimes came around. His greasy, dirty coveralls seemed not to abash him at all. In fact, nothing seemed to bother him. Sometimes he was waiting for her after work at midnight; sometimes he simply said he had "something on." Oh, he was a very highhanded sort of a guy. Mary went along, protesting. But she went.

The next Saturday afternoon when he arrived at her door to take her swimming, he had a package under his arm. A box of candy perhaps? Not flowers, unless they were very short-stemmed.

"Where's the kid?" he asked. "Stevie?"

Mary summoned Stevie from his labors in the back yard. Mike stuck out his hand and pumped the small boy's grubby one. "I brought along a model plane here," he said. "I make a hobby of putting them together. I thought maybe you'd help me."

"Gee," said Stevie. "Well—I guess so."

Mike said, "When I come over tomorrow afternoon, you and I can work on it before your sister and I have our date."

"Well!" Mary exclaimed. "Don't mind me in these arrangements. I may just be here while you two work —or maybe I won't."

Mike grinned. "I'd like you to be here, please," he said engagingly. And Stevie was glowering at her as though he found her, as usual, difficult.

"I hope I won't be in the way," Mary murmured.

From then on Stevie had a pal and a hero. And Mary was sometimes half resentful that she seemed to be put in the position of third party while Stevie and Mike worked on the details of miniature planes, cars, and boats and began to sling around words that were foreign to her. Yet she was delighted that Stevie was now a boy with an interest, a boy with a pal.

Of course it momentarily irked her when Mike, driving up on a Sunday morning, asked, "Where's Steve? I want him to come help me work on my car." He acted as if he hardly saw her.

And then came the time he suggested that they take Stevie swimming with them. Naturally, Steve quite gloried in the fact that his sister was being made to feel like a tag-along.

"That Mike is a fine boy," her father said.

"If you like that type," Mary said.

"Look what he's done for Stevie, Mary."

"He doesn't do much for me," Mary said. She caught her father's quick, keen glance. It was as though he was searching her face, asking, Do you like this boy, Mary? Are you forgetting Andy? But he didn't ask. A wise father.

He was funny, this Mike. Mary found her resistance dissolving, especially since he didn't give her much to resist. He wanted to be with her, obviously; he wanted to take up most of her spare time. He was good company, an easy talker, a fellow with dynamic ideas. He wanted to take her all sorts of places for fun.

Yet he never asked or tried to kiss her during those first weeks they were together. He was nice to her, but offhand. She imagined it was the way he expressed affection for his sister, Joyce. I might as well be another sister, she told herself.

And then she added, So what do you have to gripe about? That's exactly the way you want it, isn't it, Mary Munday?

He's a wolf in sheep's clothing, she thought, watching him one day as she lay on the shore of White Sands. He came out of the water as he did everything: expertly, flashily. He shook his wet black hair with a toss of his head, walking with grace and assurance, his broad brown shoulders glistening. He just naturally looked as though he ought to be resisted. And still he gave her nothing to resist. Unless it was his self-assurance.

"That's quite a guy who hangs around after you," Stelle said, having a smoke before she left one night. "Cute-looking. Hot stuff, hey?"

"I wouldn't know," Mary said. "Not with me, he isn't. He treats me like a sister."

"Oh, go on, who you kidding?" Stelle scoffed. "A fellow who looks like that never treated anyone like a sister in his life, unless she was his sister."

"He's very fond of her," Mary said. "I think he gauges everyone by her. And I tell you, he treats me very nicely—like a sister. He makes model planes with my little brother, mostly."

Stelle went off into stitches. "Either," she said as she regained her breath, "you're as innocent as you look or this guy's got you hoodwinked plenty. Oh, Brother! What a technique he must have."

"I wouldn't know," Mary said. "And I'm not interested in his technique. He's someone who's fun to be with, and he's good for my little brother. That's all it amounts to."

Stelle was suddenly serious, her green eyes narrowing. "You're kinda unhappy about something, aren't you?" she queried, putting out her cigarette. "Kinda young to act so disillusioned, aren't you? What happened, a bad case of puppy love?"

"Nothing happened," Mary said shortly. "I've just decided I don't want to go steady with anyone."

"Someone let you down, honey? He must've been a heel, a nice kid like you."

"He wasn't a heel—" Mary began before she realized it was a slip. She colored and snapped, "I just happen to be bored with the idea of fellows right now —at least any of the ones I know."

"They're all heels," Stelle mused, gazing into space as though she were looking down long rows of fickle men. "I've met up with more varieties of no-goods in my time than you could imagine. My first husband, Frankie, looked kind of like your Mike—oh, he was a doll to look at. But mean? I didn't have to take that from any man. I learned then, you'd better be meaner'n they are or they'll two-time you every time. My second guy——"

"Excuse me," Mary said. "Number three wants his pie."

She walked away from Stelle and her memoirs. She didn't want to get involved in Stelle's romantic affairs. Poor Stelle. She had probably been hurt, as only a gone-wrong love affair can hurt, Mary thought sentimentally, and so she had become soured on all of life. She had acquired a hard veneer which she thought would protect her from ever being hurt again.

Funny thing, Mary thought, the veneer would be the very thing that would keep Stelle from ever being loved by any man who really mattered. There *are* such good men in the world, like my father, Mary thought. I *know* there are good men . . .

Because she intended to have no entangling alliances with Mike, or anyone else, she accepted a date with a fellow to whom Barbie introduced her. She and Jack Lord would double-date with Barbie and Arlie Brown for a Sunday-afternoon picnic up at Evergreen.

And when Mike asked her on Friday—always so casual, taking her for granted—what they should do on Sunday, she said breezily, "Oh, I'm sorry. I'm going on a picnic with friends of mine. Barbie and Arlie and another fellow."

Why was it that she felt a moment of satisfaction when Mike looked dashed? You can always, she said to him but not aloud, go put together planes with Stevie!

Mike recovered his *sang-froid* immediately. "Well, good," he said. "I've been meaning to take a trip up to Frazer Lake, fishing. I'll take Joyce and we'll do that Sunday then."

He didn't even try to make her jealous by mentioning a girl other than his sister. And if he cared at all, Mary thought, wouldn't he ask her quickly to reserve the *next* Sunday for him?

He was his own debonair self, coming in to eat that next week. He waited for her and took her home a couple of times. He told her about his fishing trip with Joyce. About how you have to leave the car, after driving up as high as you can go, and then hike for five miles to reach the lake. "But it's worth it," he exulted. "I got five beauties. And Joyce beat me, she got six. That sister of mine," he said, "is the best darned sport. I'd rather have her along on a hike than a fellow any time. What a girl! The guy who gets her will be getting something pretty special."

I've done my share of hiking too, Mary thought grimly; *I've been a good sport.* She hated the surge of jealousy that shot through her. What did she care if Mike praised any girl, particularly his sister? She was furious at herself, and shaken.

She mustn't show it. As she said good night at her door she sounded too gooey-sweet to her own ears.

Oooh, he made her so mad. What was his game anyhow?

"Is Mike coming over Saturday?" Stevie asked her. "I haven't seen him for *ages*. And I can't finish the Convair till he helps me."

"I don't know," Mary told him. "I'm going swimming with my girl friends. He can come over and play with you if he wants. I won't be here."

"Oh, for corn sakes!" Stevie protested. "What're you doing—fighting with him now? He's the best guy you ever brought around here. Why can't you behave?"

"I am not fighting with him! And I must say, I don't

have to pick my boy friends just because my little brother wants to play with them. *You* run around with him if you want to!"

"You know that won't work," Stevie growled. "It's you he's got a case on, though I can't think why. You ought to hang onto a guy like that."

"You hang onto him, if you want him!" Mary cried. "You're welcome to him."

She flounced out of the kitchen, where she had been ironing while Stevie ate his lunch. It didn't help a bit when, a moment later, Stevie wandered out to his father, home on vacation and weeding in the side yard, and Mary heard her brother say, "Why do you s'pose Mary hates Mike now? Criminy, girls are sure funny!"

"Hates Mike?" her father said benignly. "What makes you think she does?"

"She practically said so, just now. She got real mad when I said she ought to hang onto him. She said I could have him if I wanted him. *You* know it ain't me he wants."

Jim Munday chuckled. "Steve," he said, "you've got a lot of learning ahead of you. It'll be painful too, a lot of it. Girls don't always say what they mean."

"That's for sure!"

"And your sister," Jim Munday said, sobering, "after a pretty tough experience, is having a spell of growing up fast right now. And that's painful too. We've got to help her, Stevie, and be patient."

[136]

Mary's emotions were so mixed, as she started folding ironed shirts, that the collision of all of them caused tears to spring to her eyes. Nothing, absolutely nothing, made her so furious as to be told she was "growing up." If, after all her experience and being nearly eighteen, she weren't grown up yet——! And for her father to insinuate to Steve that she might be caring about Mike Aldo! And then she thought of the gentleness in her father's voice when he spoke of her ... his understanding.

The girls had their say too as they went to Congress Park that afternoon for a swim. Mary sat on her huge towel, her head thrown back, her eyes closed, drinking in the sun. They had been in the water for an hour and now they were resting. Barbie brought up the subject: "I like your friend Mike," she said dreamily, stretching in the sun. "He's—exciting."

Lutie, who didn't realize how carefully she had been watching a group of fellows and their antics, said absently, "Yeah. Exciting. How'd you manage this, Mary? Frankly, I'm glad you're going with him and are all over your crush on——"

Jodell, who was rubbing suntan lotion on Lutie's back, this instant slapped her smartly so that Lutie yelled, "Ow! What did you do that for?"

"Just trying to make you tingle," Jodell said calmly. "Here you are. I'm all through."

"She was just trying to shut you up so I wouldn't

be hurt by mention of Andy," Mary said. "And she needn't have bothered because I'm not hurt about Andy—any more," she added honestly, for she couldn't be otherwise with these girls who knew her so well. "And you don't have to worry about me any more, any of you, because I'm all through being hurt by anybody. I don't intend to get involved with Mike either."

"Gad," Lutie said, "give me a chance to get involved with a guy like that! I don't see how you ever snagged him, frankly. Our little, old sweetie-pie, our wide-eyed Mary-girl. She brings home the biggest bacon of them all."

"Help yourself," Mary told her, and flushed prettily when the girls laughed at her.

They also had news for her. Had she heard about Tress?

"No," Mary said. "I haven't heard from her since she called me three weeks ago. She was going on a trip to Cheyenne, to visit a cousin up there."

"She went—and she came back," Lutie said. "She's been back for a week. And she met a fellow in Cheyenne who came back down here with her on the bus. He's quite a high-flyer. I don't really like him at all. She introduced him to me at the show the other night. Anyhow, her mother simply detests him and has forbidden Tress to go with him. So——"

"All us high-flyers," Mary murmured.

"So," Jodell took up the story, "at about two o'clock this morning Tress threw rocks at my window till she

[138]

woke me up. She wanted me to come down and let her in because she was afraid to go home. She'd been out with this Randy what's-his-name. I let her in and she spent the night with me. I tried to get her to call her mother but she said, 'Let her worry. Maybe if she thinks I've left home, she won't blast me so much when I get home in the morning.' I told her," Jodell reported, "that I was perfectly happy to have her stay with me but that either she or I was going to call her mother. She said, 'Go ahead, call her if you want, but I'm not going to.' So I called Mrs. Higgins. At first she was kind of hysterical. I think if Tress had gone home right then, her mother might have been so relieved, it might have been all right. But then Mrs. Higgins began to get mad—since she knew that Tress was safe with me—and she was really telling me off when I managed to get off the phone. When Tress left this morning, she was threatening not to go home at all. I think she probably did, but I'll bet they had a real row when she got there.

"I'm worried about that girl," Jodell frowned. "It's a funny thing. I wouldn't dare say the things to my mother that she says to hers; I wouldn't even want to. And I wouldn't try to get away with all she does. My mother doesn't spend half the time hollering at me that Tress' mother spends yelling. In fact, Mother doesn't yell at me at all. I think it's because we respect each other."

"I love my mother too much to yell at her," Barbie

said softly. "She isn't strict at all; she's too busy to be strict. I wouldn't hurt her for anything in the world. But I can see how Tress would feel different about her mother."

"Perhaps it's because they're so much alike?" Mary mused. "They hurt each other because they have the same faults and the same fears, and they know where each other is easiest hurt."

"I wonder," Lutie reflected, "if that's the way it usually is. I mean, it's both the parents' and the child's fault when they don't get along. And if it's because the parents see in their child the very things they have worried about, it makes them afraid——?"

"Gosh," Mary said, "what deep talk. Come on, I'd rather be out where the water's deep and cool, man, cool!"

Mike came into Brody's that Saturday night soon after Mary arrived for work. "I've got to hurry home," he said. "The family's having a big shindig because of my Dad's birthday. We Italianos are great ones for clan gatherings, you know. Anyhow, I'd like to call for you about three tomorrow and take you up to Silver Springs Inn for dinner. Then we could ride around and end up at the Red Rocks concert. I've got tickets. It's that trio with the Civic Symphony, you know."

The nerve! Not till Saturday night—after last week's

experience—did he ask her! And he'd gone ahead and got tickets for Red Rocks . . . What to do with such a guy!

"I am not supposed," Mary said coolly, "to go to the mountains alone with any fellow. The one time I disobeyed my Dad and did, it all turned out very bad. Maybe you've heard."

"No, I haven't heard," Mike said, "but I'll talk to your father myself and tell him what the plans are. I appreciate his wanting to protect you. There are a lot of wolves around." He grinned. "He can trust me. I'll come over to see him sometime before I pick you up."

Mary opened her lips to tell him off. *What do you think I am? You're so sure, so darned sure of yourself. And of course I'm safe with you!*

But when she looked up, he was gazing down at her. She looked down again quickly.

In his dark eyes was something she hadn't seen before. Something that said, *I care for you, Mary. Please, Mary.*

....11

True to his word, Mike talked to her father, explaining exactly what they planned to do on their Sunday date, and Jim Munday agreed. Probably he thought that Mary had had trouble enough because of his previous ruling on dates in the mountains. Probably he was showing Mary that he still trusted her.

Mike picked her up at three o'clock. She had bought herself a new blue polka-dot cotton dress with a pleated skirt and ribbon-like shoulder straps topped with shoulder bows. She *knew* she looked nice.

They took the winding canyon road to the Silver Springs Inn, which stood high at the head of a beautiful mountain valley. On the way, driving at moderate pace, Mike said, "All I do, when I'm with you, is to talk about myself and my big plans. You've never told me about yourself. What college do you plan to go to, Mary?"

She was about to equivocate. But she knew she

couldn't any more. "I quit school in May," she said
flatly. "I'm not going on."

"You quit——?" He turned to stare at her. "Why?"

Mary stuck her pretty chin forward. "I'll tell you
why. You mean you haven't heard?"

"No, I haven't heard anything. I supposed of
course——"

So she told him. All of it. Now he'd know. He listened in silence.

When she had finished and sat still, awaiting some
slight change in him, some expression of disgust, he
said, "Well, that's a darned shame. But it wasn't anything to quit school about, was it?"

She flew at him, overly defensive. "I don't have to
stick around where they believe things like that about
me!"

"Who believed what?" he asked. "Gossip . . . a half-
balmy old lady, some stupid girls clattering. Everybody gossips. If you're going to worry about what
people say——!" He sounded superior. "You don't know
what it's like . . ." she began hotly.

He stopped her. "Yes, I do know what it's like. Did
you ever stop to think what it might be like to be a
member of a minority race? I'm Italian, you know. A
Dago. There are people who think no Latin ever
amounted to anything."

"No one says that," Mary told him quickly. "You and
your sister are very popular in school. You're leaders.

Your father's name is highly respected in art circles. I know, I hear him mentioned often."

"It wasn't always that way." Mike's eyes were straight ahead on the road, his hands easy on the wheel. "When my father was starting out, in a tiny shop, and we were hard up, things were different then. And when I started school—well, you may have heard gossip about me too. I think my reputation as a tough little mutt must have followed me for years, because I had to beat up almost every kid on our side of town when I started school, to convince them that I might be a Dago but I'm just as good as any of them. I convinced them," he said with quiet pride. "To my mind, nobody is better than I am because of race or creed or social position. As long as I keep my nose clean and do what I think's right, they'd better not try to tell me I'm not equal to anyone. And that's the way you ought to feel too, Mary. My mother used to tell me, '*Non quello ce sia ma quella ce sia*,' which means, 'It's not who you are, it's what you are.'"

"A girl can't go out and beat up people," Mary said. "If she did, she'd get gossiped about more than ever."

"Well, of course, that's true. But that isn't all of it. It goes deeper. Most important of all, you have to *know*, deep inside yourself, that you're just as good as anybody else—maybe a little better. You have to feel that way and live that way, so you *can* hold your head up. Gosh, Mary, a sweet girl like you—why, your goodness and sweetness stick out all over you. A person would have to be blind, deliberately blind, not to know what you are. Down in that joint where you work, you stand out like—well, like a Bauer's twenty-five-dollar wedding cake set down in the midst of all their other crummy pastry and stuff. How's that for a simile, hey? Pretty good, that!"

"Stelle thought of the crummy part first," Mary said. "Well, there's one thing I'll grant you: you don't lack for self-confidence, that's for sure." She was smiling now.

He chuckled but grew quickly serious again. "It makes me mad that your feelings were hurt. But you must not have any self-confidence at all. And that's where the trouble lies. That's *your* fault. I would think just living with that swell father of yours would make you proud of him."

"But I am!" Mary cried. "Don't you see, that's why——"

"It's a funny way of showing it, letting him down by quitting school."

At first she was angry, stung to the quick. But then she thought of his words of admiration for her father, and she choked up. It was wonderful to know that someone else saw her father as she knew him to be, that someone else could see all the fine traits in him.

"And when you go back to school," Mike said, "by golly, you're going to hold your head just as high as the next person. Let anybody so much as breathe a word about my girl and I'll start punching again!"

"I'm not going back," Mary said, not facing him and not very able to hold her voice on an even keel.

"Yes, you are going back!"

"I'm not!"

"You are!"

"I'm not!"

"We'll see," he said calmly as he parked the car. "Here we are."

They had an excellent dinner in the dining room of the Silver Springs Inn, seated in front of a wide window that looked out over the whole sweep of the Rocky Mountain Range.

"The service here is a little different than the service in Brody's," Mary said. " 'Everything from shoes to nuts,' as Mr. Sippes would say. I feel like Cinderella. I feel as though I should be waiting on the waitresses! Gee, some of them look real elegant, don't they?"

"Probably most of them are college girls from the East," Mike said. "Most of these mountain resorts, you know, hire girls who want to come out here for a vacation and earn money at the same time."

"And here sits Mary Munday from Brody's hash house, giving her order. If they only knew!"

"There you go again!" Mike sounded annoyed. "See what I mean? No guts. If you don't hush that kind of talk, I'm going to have to smack you."

"Just try it," Mary urged. "You just try it. I'll show you who's got guts!"

He chortled. "That's my girl. You've no idea how cute and pretty you are when you get spunky. You ought to stay that way all the time. That's the way I like you best!"

They drove down the mountain road again, heading for the concert. Red Rocks is a vast natural amphitheater, carved out of the red rock from which Colorado draws its name. Though they had arrived more than an hour before the concert, crowds were already gathering, whole families or groups of friends, many of whom had brought picnic suppers.

Though the day had been warm, with dusk settling down the air was already cooler. Mike had warned Mary to bring something warm, and it wasn't long before a sweet, clear breeze was wafting over the entire bowl and Mary was glad to slip on her coat and sit close to Mike.

There was a beauty about Red Rocks that could not fail to enthrall even the most indifferent observer. Even without the music to enhance the atmosphere, the panorama was breathtaking.

Artists attending the summer festival in Aspen, where famed musicians assemble from all over the world, were the guest soloists who came here to perform with Denver's Civic Symphony Orchestra. As the glorious opening chords of Tchaikowsky's Concerto in

[147]

B Flat Minor pealed out, an appreciative ripple spread through the audience. More of Tchaikowsky's music with a muted violin solo followed. When the clarinetist soared to great musical heights during his performance of Norman Dello Joio's Concertante for clarinet and orchestra, Mike turned to her with shining eyes and his arm slipped around her waist.

The audience was spellbound. Mary gazed up at the miles of blue haze that spread far out over the circle of mountains gleaming whitely against the darkening sky. And below, like some fairy city, twinkled the many lights of Denver, stretching for miles. Now a long, dipping row of pale green lights—just a highway when you were on it; now a cluster of shimmering white lights—probably only a refinery when you passed it close at hand. But up here the enchantment remained.

Such an unbelievably beautiful world! Looking up into the heavens made her feel very small and unimportant and yet serene and happy, as though all must be right with the world.

The concert ended all too soon. At first there were crowds and traffic snarls with so many cars weaving out of the park and down the roads toward home. When they were well on their way, Mary and Mike were still under the spell of the evening's magic. They talked softly about the music, then fell silent.

Mike drew up before her house, his promise to her

father kept. Abruptly he turned to Mary and pulled her into his arms. There was nothing gentle about his first kiss. He was rough and thorough and his breath was warm as he held her tight. "I'm crazy in love with you," he said huskily.

Then he released her, went around and opened the car door on her side, and escorted her up to her front porch. He said good night and was gone, sliding away from the curb in his car.

Mary stood there, shaken. No, no, no. It isn't the same; it will never be the same again. The magic is gone, the sweetness. There isn't anything sweet about Mike. He's tough. And hard. He means to be that way, he's worked to be that way.

But he cares about me, she thought, brushing her hot cheek. He's tough, but he cares. I don't want him to. I don't feel anything toward him . . . But why do I feel this way inside?

I don't like it, she thought. I do feel something and I don't want to.

.... 12

It was August now, and everyone was beginning to be tired of summer, short as the season is in Colorado. Some of the days were dog days, hot and sticky. But occasionally there was a whisper of fall in the night wind and Mary, lying awake, would hear the cricket choirs begin. Always before, by this time, she had enjoyed their sound because it had meant that autumn was coming. And autumn had meant school and new, interesting events.

She had always loved school, though she may not always have admitted it. But she wasn't going to Central now.

Whatever interest she had extracted from her summer's new experiences had long since faded. She was thoroughly sick of working in Brody's. She meant, one of these days, to go back to the woman in the employment service and find out if, with all the other inexperienced kids going back to school, there would be a new and better job opening up somewhere.

August was ordinarily the month of the year when she had the most difficulty managing Stevie too. The first week after school was out in June, he and all his neighborhood pals were always a bit too exuberant— "No more teachers, no more books"—then he'd settle down, more or less, to enjoy his summertime pursuits. But by the middle of August all the youngsters grew restless, tired of the long, hot, lazy days. Though he would have bitten his tongue sooner than admit it, Stevie would actually look ahead to school and the familiar, everyday routine.

Thanks to Mike, Stevie, who had worried them and been quite fractious earlier, was now so busy that he had no time to hang around after dark, or to raid neighbors' fruit trees, fight with other boys, or tease the screaming, tattling neighborhood girls.

Stevie and Mike were engaged right now in the big project of building a Hi-Fi record player. The basement became a hodgepodge of old radios and all kinds of parts.

"The microphone works like your own ears," Mary heard Mike instructing. "It has a diaphragm that vibrates when a singer's voice hits it. The microphone has a crystal that changes the movements of the diaphragm into corresponding electrical signals——"

And Stevie, who could look remarkably blank when given a simple instruction about work, appeared to be eating up every word. None of it made any sense to

[151]

Mary, but Mike's and Stevie's talk became punctuated with such strange words as capacitators, power and matching transformers, inductance coils, phonograph pickups, amplifier tubes, rectifier tubes . . .

"Where's Steve?" Mike demanded, coming into the kitchen one day. He was smiling broadly as he gazed at her with shining eyes. Because she looked cute in her blue shorts and halter, her hair in a high pony tail. Because he liked her. "I've found a radio with the right type of power transformer!" he breathed at her ecstatically.

"Well, bu-lly for you! He's in the basement," Mary snipped. "Find your own way. I'm leaving!"

"Oh," Mike said, starting for the stairs, "I thought maybe we could go swimming later."

"I'm going sunbathing with friends," Mary said, being very aloof. "And I have no idea when I'll be back. I hope you two will be very happy together."

The trouble was that, though there was a tiny glint of amusement in his dark eyes when he got her pique, he let her go without argument, just kept on his course down to the basement to find Steve. The man needed killing.

Still and all, how could she quarrel with a fellow who was doing so much for her brother and thus for her and her father?

But she did quarrel.

In the first place, it was as though Mike—having, for reasons of his own, held himself in check for the first month or two—had now loosed his feelings for her so that he was quite demanding when they were together. He was a good companion, and fun too. He took her to all sorts of nice places: Red Rocks again, out to dinner both in town and in the mountains, swimming and to the movies, Elitches, Lakeside, and the Country Club for dancing, up to Central City to see the hit play with a troupe out from the New York stage. But he was very possessive, and on the way home he would want to hold her in his arms; he would kiss her roughly.

And Mary was resisting all the way. She was afraid of him, afraid of caring again. She tried to keep him at arm's length, but she didn't always succeed.

Furthermore, Mike would not let her alone about going back to school. They argued the subject hotly.

Sometimes he tried guile. One day he had with him a pamphlet he had picked up, *Occupational Guide*, put out by the Special Services Section of the State Employment Service. This one was on the subject of airline hostesses.

"You see, you need to have either two years of college or a registered nurse's certificate, or three years of business experience in public-contact work—besides a high school diploma," Mike began earnestly.

"Well, I qualify for the public-contact bit because

[153]

of my job at Brody's," Mary said fliply, but he ignored her and went on. "Listen to the swell deal you get . . ." He began to read from the bulletin: "An absorbing modern career with a chance to enjoy localities never before visited. You're apt to be stationed in a sea-board city where flights originate . . . 'the starting salary is a hundred and eighty-five dollars a month, and an hourly rate in proportion for excessive flying hours' . . . when you're away from base on duty due to flights, you usually get your living expenses paid besides a dollar a day for incidental expenses . . . and here it says that the 'turnover rate is high since continued employment is conditioned upon hostesses' remaining unmarried and the marriage rate is high.'"

Mary sniffed. "That's a scurvy bit of propaganda. Trying to bribe girls into joining so they'll get a man. Like 'Join the Navy and See the World'—and Tress' brother spent his whole hitch in a recruiting office. If I ever got into such a deal, it would be because I wanted to succeed in a career. I'm not looking for a man. And a job offer that leads eventually from my kitchen into another kitchen doesn't tempt me."

"You don't mean that!" he said irately. "What are you trying to do, model yourself on Stelle? That's who you sound like. And it sounds phony as the dickens, if you want to know. If I believed some of the things you say, instead of judging by the way you look and act, I wouldn't stick around, I can tell you."

"Well, that's just too bad," Mary told him. "Pardon me while I fall to my knees and beg you to stick around. If I did go back to school, you wouldn't notice me anyhow."

Suddenly he turned and, seizing her by the shoulders, began shaking her. "Will you cut it out?" he said angrily. "You—crybaby!"

She pulled away from him and started to get out of the car—they had parked near one of the lakes in City Park. He grabbed her and held her in her seat. He didn't act, now, as though he had any inclination to take her in his arms. He was just holding her there, so he could fight with her. He got his wish.

"I hate you!" she cried through a sudden, appalling gust of tears. "You're—you're a big bully! You think you know everything. Why don't you leave me alone and let me lead my own life? I was doing all right till you came along!"

"You weren't doing all right at all! You were just about to louse up your life plenty, because of some stupid, childish thing. What sort of a hold did that guy Andy have on you, that you're willing to make a mess of your life, disappoint your father, and let your friends down? I'd like to give your Andy a good punch in the nose!"

"He isn't 'my Andy!'" Mary struggled. "You're hurting me. You have to settle everything by force, don't you?"

"It evidently takes some kind of force to bat ideas into your silly head!" He tightened his hold on her arms. "I think your father's too easy on you. He ought to take you over his knee!"

And then, all at once, he gazed into her blazing, tear-filled eyes and his hands loosened as he said, "Gosh, Mary, I'm sorry. I don't know what got into me."

He was still holding one arm, as though he didn't trust her, and well he might not, for she suddenly pulled away and was out of the car in a flash. Mike jumped out after her.

She began to run, stumbling in her high heels. When had she run so blindly before? The day she had rushed out of school and home, angry tears blinding her. Here she was, running again . . .

She couldn't outrun Mike. He caught up to her and took her arm again, gently but firmly. "Mary, you've got to listen," he pleaded. "I'm sorry, honest I am. It just gets under my skin to think that some other guy could do this to you, could make you so cynical and bitter . . . make you want to give up all the things a girl like you should have. You've got to come back to school, Mary, you've just got to. You're my girl and I want you in school with me. For your sake and mine too. I'm almost tempted to say I'll quit school if you don't go back, because I sure won't be very happy without you there. But I couldn't do that, it just isn't

[156]

in me. I think it's too important to go on."

She couldn't escape him so she stood very still, holding herself rigid, her face averted and cold. "Please, Mary?" he whispered, kissing the top of her head. She neither moved nor answered.

"Will you get into the car and let me take you home?" he asked. After a moment's hesitation, denoting great reluctance, she stalked to the car, climbed in, and sat stiffly erect.

He took her home.

He came into Brody's after work next night. Besides the grease smudge on his cheek, there was a humble expression on his face. She wouldn't look at him. He slipped a small package into her hand. "I'm crazy about you," he whispered as though Mr. Brody weren't standing there, taking it all in. "I'll be here at midnight. Okay?"

Mary turned away. Mike walked out.

"Looks like," Mr. Brody observed, chewing reflectively on a toothpick, "you've got yourself a guy there. You like him?"

"I hate him!" Mary snapped.

"Wouldn't have known it." Mr. Brody smiled his one-sided wintry smile. Mary secretly thought that he smiled so cautiously because he never wanted Mame to catch him at it. "I guess he's got you hog-tied."

"He has not."

There was no one in the place at the moment, so

Mary set about briskly polishing counters as though her job depended on it and as though she cared.

Just then Mame stuck her head through the kitchen door and squawked, "Mary, if you ain't busy, will you get out here and help me clean up some of these? If we don't get a boy soon, I'm striking!"

Suddenly Mr. Brody turned, looked sternly at his spouse, and bellowed, "Mary wasn't hired for that sort of thing!"

While Mary stood transfixed, Mame Brody stood in the doorway, her mouth opening and closing like a fish out of water. Then she let the door swing shut and could be heard beginning her scolding and banging among the pots and pans. "I can go help . . ." Mary whispered.

"You stay here," Mr. Brody said. "She's had that coming for twenty-seven years." The smile that flitted briefly across Mr. Brody's face was almost gay. Almost.

When Mary observed that his attention had finally settled on other things, she opened the package Mike had given her. The sweetest pair of tiny patching pins, little red cherubs, saying, "Mary, be an angel?"

He was waiting for her that night. As they drove off she thanked him for the gift, then Mike said, "My mother has asked me to bring you to dinner next Sunday. Would you come, Mary?"

He sounded so anxious. "Your folks wouldn't like me—" Mary began. She had admired the lovely old

[158]

house for many years, set on one of Denver's most dignified streets. She had often seen the Aldo name as she scanned the society page.

Now she had probably annoyed Mike again with her lack of self-confidence. But evidently he was determined to hold onto his temper. "They will like you," he corrected gently. "I've told my mother all about you. And you'll like them. My father is an explosive, opinionated fellow, but he's quite a guy. He and I have our arguments, but he won't argue with you. He'll likely fall for you himself and want to monopolize your attention. He really expands when he's got a feminine audience—any audience, for that matter—but especially an attractive feminine one. He worships Mother. We all do."

"You always speak so nicely of your mother and sister," Mary said. "I think it's wonderful when a family is like that." She could see, as she glanced at him, the pleased expression on his face. "Of course," she added, "I feel the same way about my Dad and Stevie."

"I know you do," he said warmly. "That's one of the things I most admire about you—you sort of mother your family. Sometime," he said, turning to look into her eyes, "when we've both accomplished the things we have to accomplish—to get the education that we, at least I, need to get, to support us—sometime I'm going to marry you, my little Mary, so you can be the wife I've always dreamed about, the kind of a mother I've always wanted for my children."

She cleared her throat and changed the subject quickly. "Are you more like your father or your mother?" Her voice came out unevenly.

"Oh, I'm sort of a combination, I guess. I have my father's temper, only I don't spill it all over the landscape at all hours, as he's apt to do. He's very temperamental. I just save my temper for special things—as you very well know." He grinned at her.

"Dad and I have had some fights," he went on. "We still have, but not as many now because he goes his way and I go mine. That's because he has a theory about raising kids, and in spite of himself he sticks to it pretty well. He's always said that, if you teach a child right from wrong and bring him up well until he's fourteen, then he should be on his own. Parents should just stand by to be of help or give advice if they're asked, but otherwise, from fourteen on, children should make their own decisions. He feels this way because he immigrated to this country, by himself, at fourteen. I guess the theory works, at least in our case. I know I would insist on doing my own deciding anyway, and it would only mean a big row if Dad tried to stop me. But as it is, between my respect and affection for my mother, and because both she and my father worked hard to instill the right ideas in us, I haven't disgraced them in any way. I want to please them . . .

[160]

"Another thing," he continued after a pause, "I think it helps a guy a lot to know that his folks care about each other. As high a temper as my father's got, I have *never* heard him say a nasty word to my mother. And if I ever sassed her—wow, he'd forget all his theories and knock my block off, right now. Once in a while, when I was a little guy, if I'd fuss at Mother about something, he'd sit me down in a chair and give me a stiff lecture about how lucky I was to have such a mother. His eyes would blaze as though he were preaching the gospel!"

"I wonder what it's like," Mary mused, "to hate—or at least to think you hate—your parents. Take Tress, for instance. I feel so sorry for her, and in a way sorry for her mother too. I've always been so close to my Father. We have such companionship that I feel awful when I let him down. As I did . . ." she half whispered.

He didn't take advantage of this opportunity to renew their quarrel. Instead, he reached out and circled her with his arm and held her close. And so they arrived at her house.

Mike's mother called her next day and in soft, slightly broken English asked her to dinner on the following Sunday. "We are so anxious to meet you," the mother said softly.

On Friday evening Mike brought his sister Joyce into Brody's. Mary was horrified at the sight of lovely Joyce coming into a place like this. Slumming! Joyce

Aldo was a girl you'd turn to look at anywhere, with her shining ash-blonde hair and her strangely arresting eyes, blue-gray with long, dark lashes. Her skin was a glowing ivory. She was dressed simply in a black and white sleeveless cotton print dress with a wide green sash.

Mike, with a wink at Mary, guided his sister into a booth, and they both waited, smiling, as Mary reluctantly came over. "We both want Cokes," Mike said impersonally, in case Mr. Brody was hiding in the next booth, listening. And then he said, "Mary, this is my sister. She couldn't wait till Sunday to meet you."

Joyce grinned at her warmly. "Hi. I've seen you in school and I've wanted to meet you. You are coming Sunday, aren't you?"

She was so poised, so beautiful, yet so friendly and natural. Of course, naturalness is poise. But when it is so genuine . . . Right then and there Mary made up her mind to acquire a poise equal to Joyce Aldo's. She felt somehow as though they were being very kind to little bashful Mary Munday. And yet they didn't seem to be aware of it.

And on Sunday at five, Mike came for her.

They drove out into Park Hill along wide, shaded streets lined with big old brick homes. Mary was nervous but Mike kept talking easily, and it helped. Before one of the older homes, square and definitely old-fashioned but very large, Mike stopped and helped her out of the car with a flourish. Mary gazed at the wide lawns and the ancient, dignified trees.

"Gosh," she breathed, "I'm scared."

"Don't be like that," Mike told her. "Am I nervous with your Dad? My folks are *folks* too. They'll love you. And I think you'll like them."

He opened the heavy oak door. Mary's first impression of the house was one of spacious rooms, rich, dark woods, and everything built for durability of, say, five hundred years.

And immediately Mike's mother was coming forward to meet her: a portrait of a lady with beautiful dark eyes, a coronet of gray braid piled high, and a regal presence softened by a most gentle manner.

"This is *Mama Mia*," Mike said proudly. And just as proudly, "Mama, this is Mary."

The older woman clasped both of Mary's hands in hers and said, "We are so happy to have you, my dear. Come in and settle yourself comfortably. Dinner will be served very soon."

Mr. Aldo, a rather stout man with a florid complexion and iron-gray hair, came in and greeted her. He looked slightly shorter than his wife, possbily because of his weight. "So this is the Mary who has my son going in circles! Well, I knew how it would be. He has my taste. Yes indeed!"

He patted her hand, beaming at her as Mary blushed to the roots of her hair. Mike laughed. "I told you how

[163]

he'd be, Mary!" and Mrs. Aldo said, "Tony!" and then said something quietly to her husband in Italian. *"Tu stai vergongini questa ragacza, amore mio."* ("You are embarrassing the girl, my dear.")

Evidently she was attempting to squelch him, but he sat down, smiling broadly, on the nearest sofa and patted the place beside him. Mary sat next to him.

"You will excuse me that I sometimes speak in Italian," Mrs. Aldo said. "I know it is rude, but there are some things one cannot express quite so well in English."

"Especially to Papa," Mike laughed again.

Soon after, Joyce came in the front door, lovely in a sleeveless blue linen sheath. Behind her was a jaunty young fellow, happily at ease, who was introduced as Jack Lee. It turned out that he was a Denver University student. It helped to have him there, someone else outside the family.

They sat down to a festive dinner, well served by a middle-aged woman called Ilda, whom Mike teased and whom they all treated affectionately. Besides the roast turkey and all the trimmings, they were served side dishes of antipasto and rigottoni.

Mary lost her shyness as the conversation became lively and informal around the table. Jack Lee, who seemed to have been there often before, kept them chuckling at his wisecracks. Mike and his mother devoted themselves to making Mary feel at home. At one point Mike and his father became involved in a spirited, flashing argument as to the value of abstract art as opposed to naturalistic, which Mike favored. "My son will be an engineer," Mr. Aldo commented drily to Mary.

"We hate to eat and run," Mike said about a half-hour after they had finished coffee in the living room, "but we're going to the show. Excuse us, please."

It didn't seem right to Mary to leave so precipitously. She had the feeling that she ought to offer to help with the dishes. But this would probably be a *faux pas*, what with Ilda presiding in the kitchen and everything seeming to run with such efficiency.

Mike bent to kiss his mother as they left. And when Mary put out her hand to Mrs. Aldo, the woman drew her down and kissed her on the cheek. "Come again, Mary. We'd like so much to have you."

Mr. Aldo saw them to the door, patting Mary's arm, urging her to come soon, and reiterating that Mike had his father's good taste.

"Was it so bad?" Mike asked once they were in the car.

"Oh no! They're wonderful people," Mary said. "I don't blame you for being proud of them and your home. I had a lovely time."

"We're going to have a home like that someday," Mike told her. "Maybe not in such a big old mausoleum—though I think that house fits my family—we'll have one of these split-level jobs, I think, built 'way out, south of Littleton, where we can get a view of the whole Rocky Mountain Range, from Pike's Peak to Long's Peak. I could sit right down and draw the plans now. It will be a suitable frame for the wife I'm going to worship, just as our house is a natural setting for my mother. She's a peach of a girl, don't you think?"

"I can hardly refer to her in that way," Mary said. "She seems much too dignified for that. But she's charming and beautiful."

Mike nodded, a satisfied gleam in his eye. "You see why I've been looking for a girl like you," he said.

....13

And then, finally, it was the Sunday night before school was to open on Wednesday.

And on their date Mike and Mary scrupulously avoided all mention of school or of Mary's plans. They went to the show. Mike seemed quiet . . . could wistful be the word? . . . but he was pleasant and gentle with her. When he kissed her at the door, he held her for a moment, gazing down at her. Then he said good night and went away without another word.

I'm not going back to school, Mary thought at him.

She wondered . . . Andy was back in town by now. Would he look for her? He hadn't called. Of course not. She was a forgotten issue in his life, as he was in hers.

The girls had argued with her a lot. But she had argued back. They hadn't given up. But neither had she.

Her father said nothing. But she noticed on Sunday

that he looked troubled. She almost went to him and said . . .

But no.

Wednesday morning came, after Labor Day, and the Denver schools opened for the year. A brisk, bright morning, the kind of day that makes you long for new things, exciting things.

Mary went to work cleaning her cupboards, taking down dishes to wash, tearing off shelf paper, scrubbing vigorously at the white wood. Most girls her age were buying new schoolbooks that day. Mary was putting up new shelf paper!

There was a big emptiness inside her, a lost feeling, as though she had now, for sure, burned every bridge behind her and the crackle of the flames and the smell of the smoke were making her ill.

Jodell, Barbie, Tress, who had made up with her mother, and Lutie, preparing to go up to the state university. Mike . . . Andy—she realized suddenly that she had put Mike before Andy in her thoughts—everyone was in school, rushing through the halls, arranging schedules, gaily greeting acquaintances and teachers. And here was Mary Munday, doing housework, going to work tonight at Brody's.

Mike would give her up today. She had undoubtedly lost him now, he'd be so disgusted.

So?

She wondered if Mrs. Donner would think of her

today. But of course not. Mrs. Donner would be too busy helping many others get started in another year of school.

She worked like a dog that day. After the cupboards, she scrubbed away at the hated ancient woodwork. She was exhausted by the time she went to work that night. Exhausted and in a bad mood.

She had just finished waiting on the customers in the second booth, the only ones in the place, when Mr. Brody spoke quietly. "Mary." She looked over at him and he tossed his head, beckoning her. What had she done now?

"Mary," he said, "why don't you go back to school?"

She was startled and she felt the color surge into her face. "Are you going to fire me?" she asked, unable to think of anything else to say at the moment.

"If it would help, I would," the man told her. There was no sourness in his face now, no crankiness in his voice. His eyes were very kind. "Mary, you're the nicest kid we ever had working in here. You've brought us customers and you've toned up the place. But you don't belong here. You know it, I know it. You belong in school with your friends . . . with that Mike Aldo who's so in love with you. You've got a good mind and a mighty nice personality. You've got a future. There's no future for you here, you can see that. In fact— Mary, you're fired!"

Mary stood there, her head down, struggling with

too many emotions to put into words. She could flare up and be mad, the way she had met so many crises in the months past. But that unwonted light in the little man's usually apathetic, expressionless face, and the kindliness in his voice, hit her all in a heap. She could face up to the others, from whom she'd expected argument. Her defenses were suddenly all down now, partly because they'd been crumbling into sorry dust all day as she felt so alone and left out.

Finally she found her voice. Managing a wavery smile, she raised her head. "Fired from my first job!" she quavered through tears. "How does that sound?"

The man put his hand on her arm. "If ever you want a job like this again—God forbid!—or any other job, I'll give you the best recommendation you could ask. Go back to school, kid. Tomorrow. But I hope you'll stop by once in a while."

Mike didn't call for her that night. So he was angry. Well, at least she wasn't *starting* school again because of a fellow—the way she'd quit.

When she arrived home, her father was sleep in his big chair. She stood for a moment in the doorway, gazing at him. His head had fallen to one side, his mouth open a little. The drawn lines of his face, softened in slumber, and everything about the relaxed lines of his body, made her heart ache. She wakened him gently.

"Daddy!" She dropped to a sitting position on the

floor beside him. He opened his eyes, with a slow, pleased smile at sight of her. "Guess I dropped off," he mumbled, stretching, and rubbing his eyes.

"Daddy," she said, "I'm going back to school."

He stared at her a moment, sleepily uncomprehending, and then a great smile broke over his face. He reached down and put his arms around her. "Oh, Mary, Mary, I'm glad. Your mother and I are so glad!"

"But I'm not going tomorrow," she said, brushing tears from her cheeks.

"Well, I suppose you'll have to give the Brodys a little notice. But that shouldn't keep you from starting right in. We can manage the work here at home, Steve and I, so you can . . ."

She smiled at him. "I was fired from Brody's tonight," she said. And then hastened on to explain.

"And to think," her father mused, "of all the suspicious and unfriendly thoughts I've had about that man all summer. 'You never can tell,'" he quoted, "'by the looks of the shell, what kind of a nut's inside.' I'm going in there tomorrow and shake Mr. Brody's hand. I never trusted myself to go near the place before."

"I thought you'd be prowling around all the time," Mary said. "I was surprised that you never once came near the place."

"Oh, I drove past often enough," her father admitted. "But I wouldn't go in. No, Mary. I figured it was your problem and your decision all the way and I mustn't interfere at all. I figured"—he smiled at her with all his love reflected in his eyes—"I figured my little Mary would come through all right."

"The reason," Mary said quickly, determined not to cry again, "the reason why I'm not going back tomorrow is that I'm going downtown and spend the day buying some clothes that will knock their eyes out! Don't look so alarmed, Daddy. I mean really good things, things like Joyce Aldo wears. Nothing showy —just simple things that look expensive. I know you think that's—what's your biblical word—*vainglorious*? But I can't help it. I know I'll have to go back to making my own clothes again. And I know now they weren't so bad. I'm not ashamed of them any more, at least not of most of them. I'm ashamed that I let some feather-brained, flippety-tongued girls bother me. But this I've got to do, for my own satisfaction. I'm going to *buy clothes!*"

Her father chuckled and tousled her hair.

She spent the next day in the Denver stores. She had a grand time and didn't spend as recklessly as she had thought she might. She bought two lovely skirts, one a rather sheathlike blue plaid and the other a beautiful wool in large squares of red and gold and blue. She bought several tailored blouses and a frilly one, and a rich blue sweater set. There was a heavenly blue velveteen bolero with high pocket flaps that she couldn't resist; a luscious red wool jersey with a Peter Pan collar. And the short charcoal flannel coat she'd been wanting. She'd pick out her dancing dress later.

The phone was ringing when she got in the door at a little after five-thirty that afternoon. "Hey!" Mike said. "Where've you been? I've been trying to get you. I just called Brody's and they said you'd quit. He wouldn't fire you, would he? He sounded sore at the whole world. Mary, this doesn't mean——?"

There was such eagerness in his voice.

So mary went back to school.

Her friends, Jodell, Barbie, and Tress too ("I've won the right to have a mind of my own around our house," she announced. "And I've promised not to abuse the right.") arrived in a phalanx to proudly escort her that Friday morning.

She felt self-conscious as she entered—with a tiny thrill of gladness—the halls of Central that day.

Some kids smiled or waved or came running over to greet her. Others rushed past without noticing. It occurred to her that many students in this big school didn't know her and cared less. It was a comforting thought which put her in her place.

She faced what she'd known she had to face. Yes, she had to take the classes of last semester over again. The registrar was not tactful about it; in fact she was quite snippy. But Mary felt that she had it coming.

And then she went in to see Mrs. Donner. Chic in a green jumper that did wonderful things for her red hair, the young teacher beamed at her. "I knew you'd be back," she said in her crisp way. "You aren't really the quitter type. Though for a while it did look as though you were determined to try to prove the gossips right."

In her eyes there was a look that made Mary want to climb mountains, wade torrents, even write themes, for her.

And Mike, taking her out for a Coke briefly that night, held her in his arms and said, "Gosh, Mary, I'm so happy. I'm even glad you have to repeat a semester, for now we can graduate together."

....14

It wasn't so easy at first. Besides registering for classes, there was facing each instructor with the honest admission of the circumstances. One of them, Mrs. Bailey, said, "Well, I'm so glad you came back, Mary." A couple of others showed by their actions that they were now alerted for signs of character failure and temperament.

She met Mrs. Harrison, the cooking instructor, in the hall, the second day, and the woman said, "Oh, Mary, I hope I'm going to have you in my class." Suddenly Mary knew she'd like to take the cooking class, that she'd like to get new ideas for dressing up her table and her food. She thought of Mike's mother and her gracious home.

It was Edie North herself who came up to her one of those first days and exclaimed, "Mary, what an adorable dress! Did you make it yourself? Gee, I wish I could sew like you can!"

For an instant, there were so many things that

popped into Mary's mind to say that they would all have come out in an explosion had she let them. "No, I didn't make it," she might have said, "I bought it at Montaldos." Or—she toyed briefly with the idea—she could have told Edie of the overheard conversation last spring. She could have gone on from there with some of the bitter things she'd thought about Edie and those other gossiping girls.

But, after a second, she merely said, "Thanks," and walked on, feeling good inside because she'd won the day.

She was put on a committee for the first "Heels-and-Hose" Dance of the season. And Joyce Aldo offered to put her name up for her riding club—something that had always been one of Mary's dearest ambitions because she loved horses and had ridden occasionally at one of the stables east of town, when she'd had the time and money. She told Joyce she couldn't afford either time or money now. But when Jim Munday heard about it, he insisted that she join. "This is your last year of high school, Mary. You're going to have some fun."

Joyce seemed determined to be with her, and Mary liked the girl very much. There was no having to "keep up with the Jones" when she was with Joyce, for the girl's tastes were as simple as Mary's own.

Something else happened, a few days after the opening of school.

Mary was sitting on the south lawn of Central, studying for a test and waiting for Barbie, when she became aware of footsteps approaching. She meant to look up when she came to the end of the page but before she did, within the range of her vision she saw a pair of shoes—men's size—stop before her. Her gaze traveled slowly upward. There was Andy.

"Hi," he said. "Mind if I sit down beside you?"

"I don't own the grass," she said politely. "Help yourself."

He was ill at ease. "Mary," he said, dropping down beside her, "I sure was tickled when I heard you'd come back to school. I've—I've been gone all summer, you know, working in Wyoming. Got back just before school started. Mary, could we go out Friday night, like we used to?"

Here again there were things she could say. For instance: "I'm the same girl, in school or out of school. I'm the same person, gossiped about or not gossiped about. If I've changed at all, it's that I've learned a lot about loyalty and disloyalty."

Again she withheld all comments, amazed at how calm she felt, how objective she was about the whole thing. "I'm sorry, Andy," she said. "I have a date Friday night."

She would have been less than human if it hadn't braced her to say that, quietly as she did.

"Saturday . . . ?"

She shook her head. "I'm pretty busy."

"You're going with Mike Aldo, aren't you?" he said, looking bleak.

"We're friends," Mary conceded.

Andy got to his feet. "Well, it's nice seeing you," he said, and wandered away.

Mary gazed after him. Mentally she pinched herself, because all the feeling of hurt was gone. She was glad, for the sake of her own pride, that he had come back and asked her for a date. It was a test of something—and she'd passed it with a straight A.

It wasn't anything that had to do with Mike. Right now there was no comparison in her mind. It was as if she'd held up last year's dress, which she'd outgrown and no longer cared to wear. She marveled: last spring she had been so stirred by his high-held head, his self-assurance. Now—perhaps because he was feeling sort of foolish—he seemed to walk just like an ordinary fellow. She grinned to herself suddenly as she remembered how she and the girls had decided that, when Robert Mitchum rises and walks either away or toward the screen, just that swagger of his does things to the feminine heart. There was nothing of Robert Mitchum's walk here.

She thought Andy had looked—well, sort of average. His hair was bleached from his work in the blazing summer sun, and it looked odd in contrast to his tan, which was already fading. Perhaps now she was subconsciously comparing him with the darker, huskier, more assured Mike.

Anyhow, Andy did nothing for her.

Later Barbie repeated a conversation she'd had with Andy. He had seemed very resentful and hurt, Barbie reported. "I knew," Andy said, "when I thought of her going out with somebody else, that I wanted her back. There aren't many girls around like Mary. But she's through with me."

And so Mary's senior year began. Began again, one should say, but this time she was more conscious of it all, more aware of the opportunities and responsibilities of being a senior at Central.

The days rushed on, busy days, happy days. The usual ups and downs of school life . . . sometimes too much studying, a teacher's sharp criticism, a difference of opinion and a sudden flurry of hurt feelings here, or there . . .

But somehow, though Mary didn't stop to analyze or even think about it—she was too busy—she moved through the weeks feeling things more deeply than she had before. There seemed a new meaning to life, as though she had come alive. She was, of course, glad, down in her heart of hearts, that she was back here where she belonged . . . where she had wanted, all the time, to be.

Mrs. Donner gave a theme assignment: "An Interesting Character I Have Known." Mary wrote about the three old ladies of Brody's restaurant neighborhood. She painted them quite vividly, for she remembered them with much sympathy and affection.

Mrs. Donner read the theme aloud to the class. "This is some of the best writing that has ever been turned in to me," she said. "Class, can't you just see those three old ladies? Haven't they captured your imagination?"

And to Mary she said, "You know, there is a well-known play that had a long run on Broadway, *Ladies of the Corridor*. Your theme is just a sketch, of course, but your characterization of lonely women is a work of art, Mary."

Mary and Mike stopped in at Brody's one Friday night and held an Old Home Week session. Even Mame, in her own back-handed, grudging way, made her welcome: "That new girl ain't worth her salt"— Mame sniffed loud enough for the new girl to hear— "the customers complain all the time. You had 'em spoiled, Mary."

In the school cooking class they planned menus and prepared them. They arranged for a special lunch and Mrs. Harrison said, "You may invite your boy friends —or a girl friend—and let them see what kind of cooks you are."

There were to be four couples. The girls planned the menu on Thursday for lunch the following Thursday. It was necessary to accomplish a lot in advance because the class period each day was only forty-six minutes.

They would start the meal with a fresh fruit salad; after that there would be barbecued chicken and baked potatoes with the centers scooped out, mashed, and then put back in the shells with a dab of cheese on top, broccoli in lemon butter, hot rolls, a relish, iced tea or milk, and then for dessert cookies and strawberry sherbet. They were to prepare everything from scratch. The relish had been made several weeks before, along with other things the girls would be canning all fall.

Mary knew now that this was a wonderful class. They were learning to be experts, not only in the preparation of all kinds of food but in planning balanced menus and careful budgets. Later, Mrs. Harrison told them, they would have lectures in comparing the cost and nutritive value of the packaged foods with what they were doing now, "building" everything themselves.

On Tuesday they made the cookies so that they would be out of the way. On the day before the luncheon they prepared everything they could: setting the rolls, making the barbecue sauce, and getting the chickens ready to stay overnight in the refrigerator.

When the sherbet was ready to freeze, they set the table. Their centerpiece was an arrangement of golden mums from one of the girls' garden. These matched beautifully with the gold-rimmed china. Paper lace doilies for place settings were used, with linen napkins. Crystal goblets and shining silverware completed the handsome table-setting. When the girls had finished admiring their handiwork, they covered the table over and departed.

Mary arrived at school the next day a little before eight. This was to be a regular party, so she wore heels and her red wool jersey, bringing along her prettiest sheer hostess apron.

She rushed to the Home Ec kitchen to join the other three. They browned the pieces of chicken, poured the sauce over, and then turned on the oven. The potatoes were scrubbed and made ready, and Mary was to have charge of popping things into the oven during the period before the luncheon.

They were just about ready, and the large room was filled with mouth-watering odors, when the boys arrived at eleven-thirty. Mary was flustered, but when she met Mike's eyes she knew that, for once, *he* felt shy and the tips of his ears were red.

However, part of the training was to teach them to be good hostesses and to put their guests at ease with conversation, and they all tried. And by the time the boys had eaten everything in sight, the tension in the air had vanished and the girls accepted all compliments gracefully. "Wow, what a wonderful meal!" one of the boys sighed. "I'll never be able to stay awake for Berkley's class."

The girls had done all the serving themselves, with Mrs. Harrison appearing only two or three times to be sure that everything was all right.

Mary walked home from school alone that afternoon, for each of her friends was tied up with some activity and Mike still worked at Roadman's after school. Mary slowly scuffed along in the falling leaves, and thought long thoughts.

All through the luncheon Mike had tried to make her meet his eyes. And in them had been a special message: This, he seemed to be telling her, is how it will be in the future when you prepare my meals. This is how it will be when you are making a home for me, the home of my dreams. This is how it will be when we are married.

And Mary was frightened. It was all going too fast for her. She felt she must be a mousy little creature, set to take off behind the wheel of one of the high-powered cars Mike fancied, or a jet plane.

She must do something about this.

....15

Her father talked to her about college one Saturday morning in late fall. "Last May I started putting aside a little each month against the time when you'd be ready to go."

"How could you know that I'd want to go?"

He smiled at her gently. "You do want to go, don't you?" he asked.

"Yes," Mary said. "I guess that the little savings account I accumulated over the summer was always meant for that."

"Don't worry, we'll manage," he told her, his eyes warm with content. "And we'll manage so that you can have a good time too."

"We'll manage," Mary repeated, her smile answering his. "I think I'd love to do something like work in the university library."

And underneath it was as if a spark of resentment and resistance had been rekindled against Mike. *I'm going to college,* she told him, *and you aren't going to stop me by making me care. I'm not going to become involved with any more caring. Let me alone now.*

She must tell him this on their date that night. She, mousy little Mary Munday, must face up to him and tell him that he was too overpowering and that she didn't want to be overpowered.

It was a beautiful sunny day, so warm for early November that Mrs. McDrey was able to sit out in the yard in her big wheelchair. Home from the hospital now for two months, Mrs. McDrey was relearning the use of her limbs. "She's learning to smile too," Stevie had commented. "And that's using new muscles she never knew she had."

Mrs. McDrey's sister now lived with her and took care of her, the Munday family helping out wherever they could. Mary went over and sat with the old lady for a while that afternoon. And as they chatted lazily, Mrs. McDrey used her new accomplishment, a little smile for Mary. "You've been so good to me," she said. "I'm glad I learned to know my neighbors. Maybe, maybe the Lord meant for me to learn, through my illness, just how much I was missing. Like—like that old reprobate, Saul, when he was struck down on the road to Damascus, I, too, have seen the light, Mary!"

There was that smile, again, with even a touch of mischief in it. "We needed to get to know you too," Mary told her gently.

They went to the show that evening, she and Mike. They were both very quiet, Mary with the loaded message she meant to give him afterward.

After the show Mike drove directly to Cheesman Park, where he stopped the car on the upper road near the pavilion. *Go ahead and park*, Mary told him, but silently. *You've got a surprise coming.*

"Mary," he said, "I want to talk to you."

Mary waited. She wanted to talk too, but that could wait.

He turned toward her, though he kept his hands on the wheel. His eyes were shining very dark in the moonlight.

"Mary, I love you," he said. "I'll love you all my life. And I want to marry you."

"No, no!" Mary protested quickly. "You mustn't say that. I want to talk to you too . . ."

"Listen to me, Mary. I've talked this all over with my mother and I've planned just what I want to say. You see——"

He put one arm around her and he began to speak very slowly: "You see, Mary, I'm a guy who knows my own weaknesses and my own strength—I think. At least, I know what I want, and I know what I must do to get what I want. And one thing I know I must not do is to lose my head. You're everything I've ever dreamed of finding. You're little and cute and sweet, and you've got an honesty and an idealism about you that makes you—well, pretty special, with that swell Dad of yours and his wise ways . . . and your own natural goodness. You're more than I've ever dreamed of finding, Mary.

"And yet when I look at you—and you're so cuddly —I see that innocent, clear look in your eyes and I could go crazy I want you so much.

"And I know this won't do, Mary. We've got a year of high school ahead of us, then we'll be separated all through college, except for vacations. That's a long wait, but it's a good thing, in a way. It will test us both—and it will help us to keep levelheaded. Because we must keep our heads. That's what I wanted to say, Mary. That's what Mama and I talked about.

"I'm not even asking you now"—his arm around her tightened—"to marry me. Maybe you'd say no, but I'm telling you I'm going to marry you. Whatever it takes to make you want me, I'll do it. But meantime I want to do everything in my power to protect you—from myself, from anything that would hurt you. You're the other woman in my life who's going to be worshiped as I worship my mother.

"And so let's keep our friendship something special, something fine. And if ever I seem gruff, or you don't understand me, that will probably be the time when I'm loving you so much that I know I'd better hang on tight. But never, never think that anything I might do is because I've stopped loving you. I'll always love

[187]

you. Mama said that perhaps it was a shame we had met so soon when we have so far to go. But I said no, we're going to be good for each other.

"Maybe, sometime, we can be married during college. We'll see about that. But for now—Hi, Friend Mary."

He drew her to him and kissed her. One sweet, quiet kiss. And then he held her close and they gazed out over the park, to the lights of the city below. They sat very still, their hearts beating fast.

There had been another moonlit night in this same park. Last spring. A boy had kissed her then, one sweet, clean kiss. And then he had held her so. And their hearts had thumped like this.

And then that boy had taken her home as she knew Mike would take her home—safely, to dream sweet dreams.

That moonlight had been the paler glow of early spring. This was a golden harvest moon.

That boy had been a good boy, a clean boy. The person beside her was already a man, a strong man. Just as the moonlight was fuller, richer, so now Mary felt that her life was fuller and richer.

She had learned so much in the past months. She had learned how to be hurt and how to recover. She had learned how to face things—perhaps she had learned to stop running away. She had become more tolerant. She felt she had become a woman. Now that she believed this, she could on and be strong, stronger. She could stop resisting all of the things she had feared.

There was a sort of a melody in her heart, a melody of happiness. It was not that first breath of shy, budding happiness she had known last spring. This was a deeper kind, and her heart was very full.

She thought that she loved Mike too. She need no longer be afraid to analyze her feelings, to face life and a man like Mike. He would help her.

And there was something within herself now that she trusted. Suddenly she thought of the night in the moonlight at Red Rocks. She saw again all that wide stretch of beauty all about her, and heard once more that inspiring music. And the song in her heart now was like the music of that whole performance.

Perhaps, she thought, you have to learn to provide your own background music in life. You have to have a song in your own heart before you are ready to see the beauty around you.

When she crept into bed that night, she turned on her radio. And a man's deep voice was singing:

> " 'I feel glory in the air—
> There must be a God
> Somewhere . . .' "

Yes, Mary Munday thought, I, too, feel a glory in the air, and that glory belongs to me because I'm young and have dreams and ideals and love. I must always hold it high, for myself and for those who care so much. I will never lose it.